The House

In

The Pines

A World of Gothic – East Texas

by

Janis Susan May

BONUS MATERIAL

Chapter One – THE DEVIL'S PROMENADE
by Alicia Dean
a July 2016 release
Chapter One – RAVEN OF BLACKTHORN
MANOR by Gemma Juliana
to be released 8 September 2016

This Book is Dedicated to

Justine Gentry

beloved aunt and, more importantly, cherished friend

and to

CAPT Hiram M. Patterson, USN(Ret)

the most wonderful man in the world

Books by Janis Susan May
The Avenging Maid
Family of Strangers
The Devil of Dragon House
Shadowed Legacy
Passion's Choice
The Jerusalem Connection
The Egyptian File
Inheritance of Shadows
Lure of the Mummy
Timeless Innocents
Welcome Home
Miss Morrison's Second Chance
Curse of the Exile
Echoes in the Dark
Dark Music
Quartet: Four Slightly Twisted Tales
Lacey
The Fair Amazon
The Other Half of Your Heart
The Fortunes of Love
The House in the Pines

Books by Janis Patterson
A Killing at El Kab
Murder in Death's Waiting Room
Murder and Miss Wright
The Hollow House
Beaded to Death
Exercise is Murder
Murder to Mil-Spec (anthology)\

Books by Janis Susan Patterson
Danny and the Dust Bunnies (childrens)

Written with Aletha Barrett May
The Land of Heart's Delight (memoir)

Chapter One

CONTRARY TO WHAT too many people believe, Texas is not all desert and cacti and cowboys in boots and hats the size of patio umbrellas. East Texas is heavily forested and, to one used to California spaces, almost claustrophobic. I didn't care about that, though, for one singular thought filled my mind and my vision.

Wolfe House.

At last I was here.

I stopped dead on the white crushed rock driveway and looked up at the enormous place in front of me. Wolfe House.

The pictures of it had been impressive, but the actuality was literally awe-inspiring. Surrounded by a wide green lawn fringed with encroaching trees, it was at least three stories tall and much larger than I had expected. A great apron of a porch ran around it as far as I could see. There was a round turret with a pointy, witch's hat roof at one corner. Gingerbread dripped from every horizontal surface, and everything was sparkly white, as if it had just been washed. On the porch was white wicker furniture and flowers in large pots. Somehow the house should have looked more sinister, more unfriendly, not as wholesome or welcoming, but perhaps that was colored by my emotions. The place looked impossibly perfect, like something right off a travel brochure or cloying greeting card.

"My God," I breathed in awe.

"Impressive, isn't it?" Ryan Cable said dryly, closing my car door behind me. He had met me at the Longview airport and brought me to Wolfe House. During the amazingly short journey he had said nothing, but had driven like a maniac down the narrow, tree-lined highways, as if anxious to deliver and so be rid of me. He had gingery-brown hair and rough-hewn features that some might consider handsome. He wore an expensive suit that probably cost as much as I earned in a month. I had never seen his eyes, which sort of disturbed me. One could learn so much about a person from their eyes, but his were covered in expensive aviator-style sunglasses.

Right now I hardly noticed him though; at this close angle the house was both impressive and monstrous. Pulling my gaze away was difficult, but I managed and turned toward the back of the car.

"Your luggage will be brought to your room, Mrs. Grayson," he said, then extended his arm as if we were at a formal dance. "Mr. Wolfe is waiting for you. He asked that you come to him as soon as you arrived."

I didn't take his arm, but instead went up the stairs on my own, head held high, back straight, as if going into battle. What little I knew of the aged Mr. Wolfe – arrogant, selfish, dictatorial – fit right in with this demand. Imagine having someone fly halfway across the country and not even giving them a chance to freshen up! Luckily I didn't give a flip about how I looked and had used the ladies' room before the plane landed. Forewarned is forearmed.

Suddenly my thoughts were jerked in another direction. The cowboy of my early Texas imagining, complete with impossibly handsome face, huge hat and tall boots, strode around the porch and, giving Mr. Cable the briefest of nods, down the stairs to the car. The only thing that kept him from being the embodiment of a romance cover model was the fact his shirt was buttoned. Pity.

Behind us the car started and drove around the house out of sight.

Mr. Cable opened the door for me. Almost a parody of a Victorian door, it was mainly etched glass. Thermal glass, I found out as soon as I stepped through it; the interior of the house was air-conditioned to a temperature usually associated with mountain winters or the interior of refrigerators. After the soul-sucking humid heat outside, the cold was like a slap in the face. I had been warned about Texans and their love for air-conditioning, but had thought it exaggerated. Humph! If the entire house was like this I hoped I had brought warm enough clothes.

Not that I intended to be here that long.

The entry hall was large and stately, furnished with either genuine antiques or wonderful reproductions, but then I hardly noticed them. Aside from the muted breath of the air conditioner the house was completely silent. I could think of nothing except the man who waited for me behind those enormous double doors.

With a slightly sardonic smile, Mr. Cable gave the briefest of knocks, then threw the doors open and motioned me in.

"Mrs. Grayson, Uncle Henry."

I had seen pictures of Henry Wolfe, of course. Not many, because he didn't like the limelight, but no one as wealthy or as ruthless as he could hide completely from the camera.

None of the pictures had done him justice. Oh, the photographs had been accurate, presenting him as he appeared now – a craggy faced, hard-looking man in his seventies, clad in a suit and tie, sitting in his electric wheelchair with a blanket over his knees. What no photograph could show was the power that radiated from him like the heat from the small fire in the fireplace.

I think it was the fireplace that broke the spell. Outside it was hot enough to cook the traditional egg on the sidewalk; inside the air conditioning was so low it was all I could do not to shiver, and this man had a fire burning even as the compressor forced in refrigerated air. I felt as if I had fallen down the rabbit hole.

Later I would realize that the room was both big and impressive, furnished with large-scale antiques that were probably real. Tightly closed French doors filled two walls facing out onto the wide porch. But that was later; at that moment all I could see, all I could think about was that at long last I was here in the same room with Henry Wolfe.

My stomach started to hurt.

It was a little unnerving that Henry Wolfe seemed to be studying me as much as I was him, eyeing my jeans and simple blouse and blazer with just the slightest hint of disapproval. He was taking his time about his inventory, too, and now I knew how a prize cow probably felt at auction. His watery, pale blue eyes were piercing, penetrating, almost as if they were looking into my very soul. I tried to give him as good back, but although I have interviewed famous and powerful and even dangerous people all over the planet and was capable of holding my own even with world leaders, I couldn't seem to think of a thing to say.

"So you are Dianne O'Malley Grayson," he said at last, using my full professional name. I tried to tell myself it didn't mean anything. His voice was still strong and commanding, but tinged around the edges with the tremolo of age.

"Yes. And you are Henry Wolfe," I managed to respond. My words seemed to be sticking in my throat.

"Welcome to Wolfe House, Mrs. Grayson. Please… sit down." With a wave of his age-spotted, claw-like hand he indicated a chair opposite his own. "You have met my grand-nephew Ryan Cable?"

So he wasn't just an employee like I had thought, which had been stupid of me. Simple employees seldom had such exquisite suits or such an arrogant manner. Still it bothered me that while my research had turned up Mr. Cable's existence as part of Wolfe Industries, I hadn't found that he was a relative. Such carelessness could be costly.

"Yes." I nodded with a studied graciousness to him as he went to stand by Mr. Wolfe. "Mr. Cable picked me up at the airport."

"Of course he did. I told him to." The old man turned to look up at his grand-nephew. His expression was not happy. "And you didn't take Charley to drive for you, like I said."

"Charley had better things to do," Mr. Cable said. Standing by the wheelchair, he towered over the older man. With his crossed arms and flinty countenance he could have been a bodyguard. Maybe he was. He hadn't removed his sunglasses, and his eyes were still hidden.

"So you think you can write my life story," Henry Wolfe said, just a hint of challenge in his voice.

"Being a professional writer, I am certain I can,"

I replied easily, settling in the indicated striped satin chair. It was probably a priceless antique but it was very uncomfortable. "What needs to be settled is if you will let me."

"Let you?" His shaggy brows rose. "You've got a contract, Mrs. Grayson. You're here."

"Obviously. What I meant was if you will let me write the truth and not a dandified paean to your greatness." I tried to keep my words sweet, but an edge of sourness crept in. "You see, I don't do fiction,"

Ryan Cable hadn't moved even a fraction of an inch, but displeasure positively radiated from him. Well, tough. I didn't care about what he thought. Finally he removed his sunglasses, revealing icy blue eyes at least as cold as the house temperature. In spite of that his was still a handsome face in a slightly fearsome way, a face that would always stand out in a crowd. And, I had to admit, his body wasn't bad either.

A low rumbling crept through the room, sounding almost like the beginnings of an earthquake. Being a Californian, I instinctively looked for a safe place, then realized just in time that it was Henry Wolfe laughing.

"A real pepper pot, ain't she, Ryan? We're going to have our hands full with her," Mr. Wolfe chortled, then fell into a spasm of coughing so severe that it doubled him over and sent the blanket sliding from his lap. My research showed that he had been in an auto accident a few months previously – presumably the spur to immortalize himself in an autobiography – but there had been nothing about him still being in a wheelchair.

Ryan Cable moved instantly, kneeling beside the old man and steadying him.

"Can I do anything?" I asked, horrified that my flip comment could have produced such a reaction. The old man must be more fragile than anyone outside the immediate family knew. If I was to get what I wanted I would have to watch what I said.

Ryan shook his head, but his eyes never left the old man. Within moments the spasm passed and Mr. Wolfe straightened, aided only a little by his grand-nephew.

"Age is a stern mistress, Mrs. Grayson," he said, tucking the blanket back across his lap. "She will not be mocked."

"I'm sorry to have caused you trouble," I murmured. There was more I would have said, but he silenced me with a look.

"It's part of life, dammit, and I won't have you or anyone – " he sent a blistering glance toward Mr. Cable " – coddling me or feeding me any sentimental guff. Is that understood?"

Ryan Cable said nothing, but simply stood and dusted a bit of carpet fluff off his knee as if he hadn't even heard. One slightly curling lock of his gingery-brown hair fell forward over his eye. He didn't seem to notice that, either.

This was the old man I had expected – imperious and remote, dictatorial and cold. "Yes, Mr. Wolfe," I said, and meant it. I had no intention of giving him any quarter – not that he would have expected any.

"Vernita!" he bellowed in a surprisingly loud voice, one so strong it was impossible not to wonder if his coughing fit had been staged.

Vernita Coffey must have been standing just outside the door, for she stumbled through so quickly the last syllable of her name was still on the old man's lips. I say stumbled advisedly, for she reminded me of nothing so much as a Labrador puppy, one so young that he was unsure of how his feet coordinated. But in spite of the puppy metaphor Mrs. Coffey wasn't young by any stretch of the imagination. I would have placed her in her fifties at the youngest and, in the words of my horse-loving mother, she looked as if she had been rode hard and put away wet. Average height, plain of face and chunky of body, hair overpermed into a style that was not the slightest bit flattering, she was the epitome of a poor relation. She wore a badly-fitted dress of navy blue polyester that simply screamed 'discount store.' My research had only said the housekeeper was a distant relation of Mr. Wolfe's, but I had not been able to find out exactly how. It didn't matter; she was obviously little more than a cypher and not a force to reckon with in this house.

"Yes, Uncle Henry?" Her voice was a surprise; it was soft and mellow.

"This is Mrs. Grayson. She'll be in the yellow room. Dinner's at seven, drinks here at six-thirty," Henry barked, then turned to Ryan Cable. I had been dismissed.

Which was fine with me. I had had just about enough of Henry Wolfe for the moment.

Mrs. Coffey chattered all the way from the living room, up the stairs and into the room that was to be mine. She talked about how old the house was (1870s, originally), how it had belonged to an early lumber baron and had been built for his fancy Eastern bride who had had the poor manners to die while giving birth to a girl. She talked about how the place had fallen into disrepair until Uncle Henry had bought it for his wife, back when he was just starting to become rich, and how his wife had died not many years later. She talked about how he had spared no expense to make this house a showplace, enumerating all the wonderful things he had done as gleefully as if they had been for her.

I knew most of this already – I am a very determined researcher – but was always willing to know more. Keeping my face composed, I asked, "Didn't he have a daughter?"

A look of distaste flittered over her doughy face. "Yes. Silly girl. She ran away years ago. We never talk of her because it hurt Uncle Henry deeply." She made it sound tantamount to a felony. Then stopping in front of a door that looked just the same as the other doors ringing the huge square stairwell, she opened it with a flourish as if giving me a present. "And this will be your room."

When Mr. Wolfe had said the Yellow Room, he hadn't been kidding. It was like walking into a daffodil. The walls were just a little bit too intense for beauty; thankfully they were just painted rather than wallpapered. Probably no one here read obscure Victorian semi-horror fiction, but I could see where patterned wallpaper in this room could drive someone mad. The furniture was of torturously carved dark wood, and I couldn't begin to guess from what era other than 'old'; when I had been growing up there hadn't been much money for furniture, period, let alone antiques.

There was a small fireplace too, mercifully unlit, and covered with an ornate brass screen. Two enormous windows looked out over a rolling expanse of lawn to a palisade of trees surrounding the house like defending walls.

"This is one of the nicest bedrooms in the house," Mrs. Coffey gushed, scuttling to open a door in the far wall. "And here you have your own private bathroom."

I didn't dare look for fear it too was completely yellow. Instead I casually wandered to the window and looked out. Below there was nothing but grass – no sign of a garden, or even where a garden might have been.

This wasn't it; this wasn't the room I had been hoping to find.

"I'm afraid we don't have a bell system," Mrs. Coffey babbled on. "But if you just holler down the stairwell Charley or Petunia or I will hear in case you need something."

"Petunia?"

"She's the cook. I'm afraid we have a very small staff here. There's some girls who come in once or twice a week and clean." She looked downright ashamed. "I'm so very sorry, but everyone here except Uncle Henry makes their own bed, though the girls do change the sheets every time they come."

My disappointment over the room was so great I could have wept. Instead I made myself smile cordially. "That's perfectly all right. I've made my own bed all my life."

Doubtless she would have made a reply, but instead jumped as the door slammed back against the wall. Dragging both my big cases as well as lugging my carryon and tote bag, Charley the handsome cowboy stamped into the room. He looked completely out of place, but apparently didn't care. Now I had a better look at him; dark, straight hair, light brown eyes, a jaw like a … I didn't know how to describe it, but it was square and gorgeous.

"Goodness, Charley!" Mrs. Coffey said breathlessly. "You don't have to tear the house down."

"Sorry, Miz Coffey," he said unrepentantly, then turned to me and spoke in a carefully neutral voice. "Where do you want your bags, ma'am?"

"Please put the two big ones and the carry-on over there." I indicated a vacant spot by the tall chest of drawers. "And I'll take the tote bag."

He did as I asked, smiling a little as he extended the tote bag into my reaching hands. It was a devastating smile! If he went to Hollywood he would have every female in sight swooning.

I took the tote bag carefully. This was perhaps my most precious piece of luggage, as it contained my mobile office – my laptop, tablet, camera and research notebooks. I had never let it out of my hands while traveling before, and the fact that I had spoke eloquently to my unsettled state of mind. I could only hope that none of my electronic toys had been too badly shaken.

"Well, we'll leave you now so you can unpack and maybe rest a little while before cocktails. And if I might give you a word of advice, Mrs. Grayson, do be prompt," she whispered as if imparting some great secret. "Uncle Henry is a stickler for people being prompt."

"I will be," I promised.

"See you this evening, then," Mrs. Coffey said, almost pushing Charley out the door and closing it behind them.

For the first time in what felt like days I was actually alone, and alone in this house where I had wanted to be for so long, where I could finally seek some justice.

Finally.

I would have to watch myself carefully from here on out, though, or I might say or do something stupid in a moment of inattention. That could ruin everything.

Chapter Two

"NO PENCIL AND paper, Mrs. Grayson?" Henry Wolfe asked, clinking the ice in his drink. "How are you going to write my story if you don't take notes?"

Mrs. Coffey's warning had been unnecessary. Henry Wolfe's mania about promptness was well known; it was also well known that he usually disregarded it himself. I was surprised, therefore, to find him waiting in the living room for me, in spite of the fact I was some ten minutes early.

"I have a very good memory, Mr. Wolfe. Besides, you didn't tell me you expected to begin tonight." I moved across the room to the chair he indicated and sat. It was much more comfortable than the one I had sat in earlier. It was also much closer to him.

"She's right about that, Uncle Henry," said Ryan

Cable, rising from the couch. "Plus it wouldn't be hospitable to expect the woman to start work before she gets her bags unpacked."

He had to be speaking metaphorically. I had unpacked my bags, sourly noting that while my clothes were of good quality they still looked shabby compared to the magnificence of this house. Had I been secretly hoping to find it decayed and rundown?

"Get Mrs. Grayson a drink and don't be such a smartass."

Ryan walked over to a tall, ornately mirrored bar that looked as if it had once come out of an expensive bordello. "What will you have, Mrs. Grayson?"

"A diet Dr. Pepper if you have one." I longed for a glass of wine, but didn't dare. For as long as I was at Wolfe House I had to be on the top of my game. This visit was important, and I didn't dare risk even a moment's carelessness.

"Didn't know you Californians had Dr. Pepper. It's primarily a Texas drink." He opened a can and poured it over ice, then handed me the glass.

I shrugged. "It's pretty much all over now. And I do travel a lot."

"Well," Henry said, "you're here now. How long do you think it will take to get this book written?"

"That's a question without an answer. How long and detailed do you want the book?" I smiled evilly. "And how difficult are you going to be about it?"

He glared. "As much as I want. You're being paid well for your time, Mrs. Grayson."

"I am. And I intend to earn my money," I said, not knowing if it were true or not. "I can go get my tablet if you want to start now, or we can be civilized and start first thing in the morning."

My acquiescence seemed to startle him, but he said nothing. Ryan was less reserved.

"You mean you don't intend to look around for a couple of days so you can soak up the atmosphere of the house? Get in touch with the place? Absorb the vibes?" He made it sound roughly on a par with mass murder or treason.

"I intend to do both," I answered evenly, though

it was an effort. Doubtless he had read about how some writers work, but he had struck nearer to the truth than he realized. For an entirely different reason. "But that doesn't mean we can't start work immediately."

"You'll work in my office," Henry declared. "There's a big desk in there and I can work with you."

And keep an eye on what I was writing, I added mentally. "I do need a place for my computer, and doubtless you and I will spend a great deal of time together, but I need a place where I can be alone when I write. A desk in my bedroom will serve admirably."

Henry glowered, while behind him it appeared that Ryan was either stifling a laugh or having some kind of a fit. It could have been either.

"That's not the way it's going to be," Henry said.

"That's the way I work. Besides, I think after we have been together most of the day we'll be glad for some time apart. Anyway, when I write I write alone. Take it or leave it."

Obviously Henry Wolfe was not used to people standing up to him. His color rose and he growled deep in his throat. Ryan stepped beside the old man and again I was struck by how tall and solid he was. And yes, handsome, even if it was in a rough-hewn way. Never forget handsome.

"Remember your blood pressure, Uncle Henry. And remember that not everyone does everything the same way you do."

"Dammit, I'm paying her! She should do things the way I want."

"You're hiring me to write a book for you," I returned calmly, though my insides shook. It couldn't be blowing up, not this soon, not after I had planned so long, but I had to make some ground rules. "You are not hiring me to be some sort of automaton at your beck and call. If you don't like the way I work I'll leave in the morning and we'll call this a wash."

"You have a contract, young woman!"

"Indeed I do, but there is not one word in it

about having to write this book with you breathing over my shoulder." As soon as the words were spoken I wished they could be called back. I had to stand up for my rights as a writer, but I didn't dare risk getting thrown out of here, not now, not when I was so close.

Both Henry and Ryan glared at me, Henry because he obviously was not used to having his will crossed and Ryan was telling me not to antagonize the old man as clearly as if he had spoken the words.

"I can see that this is important to you, Mrs. Grayson," Ryan said almost reluctantly. "I'll see that a suitable table and chair are put in your room."

Henry grumbled, his teeth shredding some words I probably really didn't want to hear. Ryan had laid a hand on the old man's shoulder, but his expression looked as if he would really rather have slapped it over Henry's mouth.

"Thank you. The work will go that much faster. Of course, it will be some days before I'll really start writing."

Henry's shaggy eyebrows shot up. "Think

you're here for a vacation, do you?"

"Hardly. I do have to have something to write about, though. I'll be talking to you, of course, and everyone in the household and to those at your office to start with. I'll also be doing some on-line research. I presume you have the internet in the house?"

Henry growled again, but Ryan merely nodded. "The password is lumber – all lower case."

That made sense. Lumber was what had started Henry's fortune.

"Oh, are you all talking business still?" Vernita Coffey sashayed into the room. I use the word sashayed advisedly. She had changed into a floaty, ruffly dress in a positive symphony of dismal greens, but it wasn't any more flattering than her more severe navy one. I had played it safe, wearing black slacks and a simple silky blouse of a dull gold carefully chosen to compliment my newly cut and dyed brown hair.

An imperative buzzing filled the air. Ryan dug in his jacket pocket and pulled out a state-of-the-art phone. "Ryan Cable."

Whatever was being said didn't please him. He frowned, his expression so angry I was glad it was not directed at me.

"I see… What has Carson said?..."

"Ryan, it is positively uncivilized to talk on the telephone at this hour!" Vernita scolded. "It's almost time for dinner, so hang up at once."

"Be quiet, you silly woman!" Henry snapped, then turned to Ryan. "Is there something wrong at the mill?"

Ryan made a shushing gesture with his hand, then phone still to ear, walked out the hallway door and closed it behind him.

"Young jackass," Henry grumbled. "How dare he walk away like that!"

"He's just trying to save you worry," Vernita said in a sugary voice.

"It's my company! It's mine to worry about!"

"Now don't be silly, Uncle Henry. You hired him to take some of the burden off you." Vernita patted him on the shoulders. I was surprised she didn't tell him to be quiet like a good little boy.

"Damn it all, woman, this could be important." In a less exalted human being his tone might have been called a snarl.

"Now remember your blood pressure, Uncle Henry," she said chidingly, then turned to me. "I do apologize, Mrs. Grayson. We really are a civilized family here. It's just too hard to convince these men that business has no place in the family hour."

I smiled blandly. "But business can be important, and in a global economy time frames are fluid things."

For a moment her face hardened into something arrogant and ugly, but Henry laughed. "Thought you had a good head on your shoulders, young woman. Here – fix me another drink."

I stood and took the glass he extended, ignoring Vernita's frenzied headshaking from behind his back. "What are you drinking?"

"Uncle Henry, you shouldn't…"

"Shut up, woman, and go check on dinner or something. If I want a drink I'll have one. You're the housekeeper here, not my mother."

Her face white with anger, Vernita stalked from the room, a study in frozen dignity. "I'll go see if dinner is ready."

"That wasn't nice," I said mildly once she was gone, as I added fresh ice cubes to his glass.

"It wasn't meant to be. Stupid woman. Thinks she runs things around here. Just took her on because she was my sister's daughter-in-law and she and the boy had no place else to go after my nephew Robert died." He made that act of charity sound as bad as a prison sentence.

"No good deed goes unrewarded. Now what are you drinking?"

"Bourbon. Only decent drink there is."

I kept my mouth shut on that and put a splash of liquor into his glass. "Here."

"Thank you – " he began, but once he had the glass he began snarling again. "That's not a drink! Take it back and pour me a real drink."

I smiled. "Judging from Mrs. Coffey's exit line, I assume dinner will be ready in just a minute."

"That has nothing to do with the size of my drink!"

"Perhaps not, but I don't want you to be slobby drunk. I want to question you tonight."

"Slobby!" he all but shouted, then muttered something predictable and unflattering about being the prisoner of bossy females. I paid no attention. If I was to accomplish what was necessary I had to have the upper hand at least part of the time.

"Well," he said at last, chugging down the liquid in a single swallow and shoving the glass at me, "we might as well go on in. Give me a push."

Once we got to the dining room – which was a nightmare of heavy Victorian furniture and dark red walls – Ryan didn't join us until we had finished our soup and were well into the main course of roast beef. The food had been served by Petunia, a tall, scrawny woman of indeterminate age, race and temperament. Henry introduced us; Vernita was conspicuously silent. I spoke politely, but Petunia merely looked at me, grunted, and went back to the kitchen.

"I swear, it is so difficult to get good help these days," Vernita said in a hoarse stage whisper that could probably carry to the next county. "Her manners aren't the best, but she does cook like a dream."

That I could agree with. The food was as good as I had ever had.

"Now, Mrs. Grayson, why don't you tell us a little about your family," Henry said.

It was an order, one that I had been expecting. "I was born in California, as you probably know, and grew up in a small town. My father was a mechanic and a volunteer firefighter. My mother worked as a secretary in an insurance agency. They died in an auto accident almost a year ago." Grief still grabbed at my heart, no matter how often I said it. Grief and guilt, for I had not yet forgiven myself for crying off on their invitation to go with them to dinner that night, that I had missed the opportunity of doing something – anything – to save them.

"Oh, that's terrible," Vernita said in a cloying voice. "It's hard to lose your parents."

I shrugged and tried to keep the catch out of my voice. "Yes, it is. At least they went together. They were so much in love I don't think one could have existed without the other."

Henry made a sound deep in his throat and spoke as if goading me. "What about your husband?"

Bert. A tiny stab went through me, more for lost possibilities than for a broken heart. Our short marriage had been based more on friendship – and, yes, desire – rather than real love. It could have turned into something deeper and more lasting, though, had it been given the chance. At least, I cherished that notion.

"I am sure you know my husband was a Marine. He was killed almost three years ago."

Immediately Vernita began to cluck sympathetic platitudes, but I was saved from her inevitable recital of sentimental treacle by Ryan's abruptly rejoining us.

"What a depressing subject for a dinner table," Ryan said, settling into his chair. Petunia must have had her ear to the door, for he barely sat down before she was putting a heavily loaded plate in front of him.

Then it was as if I had been forgotten, for simultaneously Vernita chided him for being so long in getting to the table, saying it was not civilized to ignore a guest, and Henry shot questions at him about the subject of the phone call like from a machine gun. I merely ate, watching the byplay with interest.

The meal had hardly ended – topped off with a slice of simply heavenly old-fashioned chocolate pie – when Henry declared that he was tired and wanted to go to bed. He had, he added with a deadly attempt at humor, to get to bed early if he was going to work with me in the morning. Ryan immediately rose and wheeled his uncle out of the room, saying he would join us in the living room later.

Which left me alone with Vernita, more's the pity. We did move to the living room, and in a few minutes a grim-faced Petunia brought in a coffee service on an enormous tray. It was, I noticed, old and probably sterling. Petunia's coffee was as good as her cooking. I had almost finished the one cup I allowed myself in the evening before Ryan rejoined us. Vernita had been chattering about all the families who lived locally – none of whom were as wealthy or as socially acceptable as the Wolfes, according to her – and the new people moving out in droves from the big cities. I was spared her opinion of them by Ryan's reappearance.

He accepted a cup of coffee, then simply sat there like a lump, studying me as if for an exam. I could think of a dozen flip remarks that would show my displeasure at being stared at so openly, but suddenly it was not only a danger to my continued presence here, it was just too much effort.

"If you will excuse me," I said, struggling to my feet from the overly soft chair, "I have been traveling most of the day and would like to go to sleep."

Vernita began to chatter again, but Ryan silenced her with a wave. "That's more than understandable, Mrs. Grayson. Breakfast is in the dining room at eight-thirty. There should be an alarm clock by your bed if you need one. Shall I walk you to your room?"

"No, thank you. I can find it. Until tomorrow, then?"

Without waiting for another word I went upstairs. With each step it seemed as if the air became clearer, less fogged by emotions and stress. It was heartening and very pleasurable.

At least it was until I entered my room, where the signs were subtle but unmistakable. Sometime between when I went down for dinner and now my belongings had been very thoroughly searched.

Chapter Three

DESPITE MY EMOTIONAL and physical fatigue, sleep was elusive. Thanks to the insulated glass the whisper of the night wind through the guardian trees ringing the house was muted and barely audible. It should have been the perfect night for sleeping, but I didn't dare.

My room had been searched. Someone had come in and gone through my possessions while I was downstairs. Oh, it had been skillfully done – the signs were so minor that in other circumstances I might not have noticed a slight rearrangement of how I had folded my clothes in the armoire, my computer being moved a little to the right, my empty luggage turned differently than I had left it. At Wolfe House, though, my senses were on such high alert that neon signs might as well have been attached to each small change.

It didn't help that in addition to being tired I was wakeful and restless, but mostly concerned about tomorrow... and tonight. So far I had managed things well, but a full day of interviewing Henry Wolfe would obviously be work, much harder work than anticipated. I would have to consciously keep my mouth shut to keep from blurting out things I should not possibly have known.

The silence of the night was broken by a sound from the hallway, a soft, nearly slithering sound like a cautious step that seemed to pause at my door. I tensed, wondering what was out there and if it intended to come in. This house had seemed haunted to me, but until now it had been the haunt of stories, of memories, and not of spooks, yet it was neither stories nor memories that stood outside my room.

I was almost to the point of rising and opening the door to confront my midnight visitor when the sound came again, this time moving away, ending with the soft closing of a door somewhere on the landing. As much as I would have liked it to be, this was not the wakeful prowling of a sleepless inhabitant or someone coming up late to bed. Those stealthy footsteps had been deliberately quiet and surreptitious.

Someone had entered my room once before; were they contemplating coming in now, even though I was in here? And what could have been their objective? I almost shuddered, then made myself relax. Thoughts like that were the stuff of bad TV movies, not reality. Events in those overwrought ninety-minute melodramas never happened to real people.

I lay staring up into the darkness, now more wakeful than ever. Who could it have been? And why? Most importantly why. The cast of characters was perforce limited. Henry was in a wheelchair, and it had been a hesitant step that I had heard, not the whirr the wheels of his chair made over the polished wooden floors. So – that left Vernita or Ryan, or perhaps Charley or Petunia, assuming they had access to the house in the nighttime hours. And who knew who else could get in, either legally or illegally?

Who – or what – walked the halls of Wolfe House in the hours of the dark? And – yet again – why?

What did they know? Or – more unnervingly – what did I not know?

The only sound in the house was the ponderous ticking of the massive grandfather's clock at the bottom of the stairs, sounding uncomfortably like a giant heartbeat. Though it was practically impossible to hear the soft night sounds from outside it was probably quiet out there, too. Everything and everybody was finally asleep.

Except me. I had lain restless in bed from the time everyone had come upstairs, listening to the soft sounds of a household readying itself for sleep – the snide whirr of the small elevator lifting Henry to the second floor, the murmured good nights, the soft snick of doors closing. When there was nothing but the faint breathy roar of the air conditioner turning itself on and off and I had heard nothing else for at least an hour, I slipped from bed and crept from my room.

In the movies when someone sneaks around in the night they always put on dark clothes, presumably to meld the better into the darkness. There was no darkness in Wolfe House; on each landing there was a series of ornate sconces with dim bulbs in them. They did not give enough light to really see by, but neither was there enough darkness in which one could hide. Well, it was what it was. Wearing the lace-trimmed robe of emerald green that was my favorite for traveling I eased the door of my room open and slipped out.

Now where did I go? The great double doors at the top of the stairs had to belong to Henry; probably a suite, as there were no other doors in that wall. Besides Henry's, six doors opened off the square hallway, two to a wall. Presumably both Vernita and Ryan slept up here, too. Three occupied bedrooms, three unoccupied, but which were which? And which was the room I wanted? If there had been any window in this hallway other than the stained glass roof, I might have been able to see where the garden ·

was, the garden which the room I sought overlooked. It was supposed to be on the south side of the house, but my command of directions was sketchy in the best of times. My only solution was to explore.

A little alarmed at how the heels of my house slippers clicked against the polished wooden floor, I stopped at the room next to mine and, putting my ear on the door, listened. Nothing. Daring to try the door, I cracked it open, but a quick peek inside revealed a room as blue as mine was yellow; empty and bland, it was obviously a guest room.

I went on around the square stairwell to listen at the next door, where I was rewarded by a snuffling, somewhat high-pitched snore. That had to be Vernita; I couldn't imagine such an effeminate sound coming from someone so overwhelmingly masculine as Ryan Cable.

That left just two rooms, one of which had to be the one I wanted. Cautiously I twisted the handle of the next room, which turned sweetly beneath my fingers.

Faint though they might be, the night sconces

threw enough light to show that this was not the room I sought. This was a man's room, severely done in browns and greens and golds. There were things – brushes, stacks of papers, a closed laptop on top of the dresser, which meant this was probably Ryan Cable's room, but he wasn't in it.

So I wasn't the only one abroad this night; but – where was he?

Suddenly panicked, I looked over my shoulder as if he might be standing there, ready to denounce me. The landing was empty, so I screwed up my courage and, closing the door, moved on to the only room left.

This door too opened without sound, and a faint mustiness trickled out. I slipped inside, closing the door behind me. The darkness was absolute; the windows must be curtained, for there was not even the slight glow of starlight. Though it was foolish, I turned on the light. After coming so far and waiting so long, I had to see.

My eyes filled with tears. This was the room I wanted to see, the room I knew as well as I had known the room I grew up in.

This was a symphony of soft pastels, pink and lilac and mauve. The furniture was light and airy, the white paint picked with gold. A golden vanity set, each piece perfectly aligned, spread across the dresser top. There were paintings, too, all pretty and soft and impressionistic. For all I knew, they were by real impressionist masters.

The only thing there I hadn't been expecting was the portrait. It hung over the delicate fireplace. The girl had been a beauty. She sat almost sideways on a spindly golden chair, her head tilted as if you had spoken and she had just turned to answer you. Her hair was dark blonde, rippling in waves down to her shoulders. She wore an expensively simple dress of pale silk, delicately embroidered at the neckline and at the edge of the short sleeves. Gold earrings glittered in her ears, but my gaze was drawn to her right hand, casually draped on the chair's arm.

Some might think that enormous, glowing red stone fringed by diamonds was a ruby, but I knew better. It was a pear-shaped red spinel, not quite as rare as a ruby of the same large size, but often more beautiful. And valuable. From the size of this one it had to have been worth a fair fortune in itself. I hadn't been expecting anything so spectacular.

"Can I help you, Mrs. Grayson?"

I jumped. The room and its contents had been so entrancing I hadn't heard the door open.

Ryan Cable stood in the doorway. This time he had on jeans and a black t-shirt that showcased his impressive musculature. I gulped, and not all out of fear.

"No," I said, hoping to brazen it out. "I'm fine."

He stepped in and closed the door behind him. Suddenly the room was much too small and I was having difficulty breathing.

"What are you doing in here?"

"Looking around. Absorbing the vibes," I said in flip tones. "You're up late."

"Just watching some television downstairs." He stepped closer, moving as cautiously as a cat. "Looking for anything special?"

I shook my head. "Just looking."

He took another step closer. Now we were less than an arm's length apart and it made me very nervous. I am not a weakling or a wuss, but it was obvious he would be stronger than I. At least, that was the reason I told myself that breathing around him was so difficult. He was a very desirable man, but his loyalty was to Henry Wolfe. What would his reaction be if he knew my secret?

His gaze left me and flicked up to the portrait as he took my chin in his hand, a touch that jolted me to the core, then gently lifted a loose tendril of my hair. "You know," he said slowly, "if you had blonde hair, and it was longer, you two would look a lot alike."

I gulped and forced a smile as he turned my head gently back and forth, studying it as would an artist. It was fear of just this kind of discovery that had made me dye my normally blonde hair a nondescript brown. "You flatter me."

"Not really. Pity your eyes are blue and not green like hers. Otherwise it would be an astonishing resemblance."

"That must be Mr. Wolfe's daughter. The one who ran away."

"You know about her?" He released my chin and put his hand back in his pocket.

"Vernita mentioned her. Do you know why she ran away?"

Ryan Cable frowned, his face darkening with an emotion I could only call contempt. "Because Stephanie was a fool. No one could tell her anything."

"But there must have been a reason... I mean, she was pampered here, had everything she wanted..."

"She was a fool," he repeated shortly. His eyes appeared as hard as the lapis they resembled. "Uncle Henry gets up early, so if you've finished absorbing the vibes, why don't we call it a night." It was an order, not a question.

He opened the door for me in an unmistakable command. As I stepped in to my room, I managed to shut the door slowly enough to see him enter his own. So I had been right; he really was right next to me, which meant he'd probably hear anytime I left.

Drat!

* * * * *

At last I slept, and so soundly that I was late for breakfast. I slid into my place. Vernita poured me a welcome cup of coffee and ostentatiously rang a little silver bell.

"I asked Petunia to keep you a warm plate," she said. "Did you not sleep well?"

"Not very," I answered slowly, sipping at my coffee. Had Ryan told them of last night? If so, everyone was taking it remarkably well. On the other hand, perhaps he was waiting until I had joined them to denounce me. I stole a glance at him, but he seemed sublimely unaware, chewing on a bite of bacon.

"Isn't your room comfortable?" Henry demanded, his strong yellow teeth snapping at a piece of toast.

"Quite comfortable. Sometimes I just don't sleep well, especially in a new place."

With considerably less alacrity and grace than

she had served Ryan the night before Petunia put a plate before me. "Purt' near dried out," she said with sullen emphasis. "Was good when it was ready."

"I'm sure it will be delicious," I replied, but the gracious words were wasted as she stumped out of the room.

"Unfortunately dear Petunia has never mastered the social graces." Vernita began, but Henry interrupted, silencing her.

"Doesn't need 'em," he growled. "She's a cook, and a damn fine one."

Even overheated and slightly dry around the edges, the cheese-laden eggs were delicious, the bacon thick and tasty. I would have eaten them even if they had been ruined. Enough attention had been directed toward me this morning, but it wasn't over yet. I had barely eaten half of what was on my plate when Ryan put down his napkin and stood.

"Ryan, sit back down," Vernita twittered. "Breakfast isn't over."

"I have to get to the office," he replied, then looked at me. "Mrs. Grayson, may I speak to you a moment?"

"Ryan, she hasn't finished her breakfast," Vernita said more strongly, even as Henry slammed down his coffee cup so hard the dark contents sloshed over onto the cloth.

"What about? There's nothing you can't say here. Let the woman eat."

"Of course, Mr. Cable," I replied, dutifully putting my napkin down and standing. Somewhat surprisingly, he pulled my chair out for me. "I really am not much of a morning eater." It wasn't totally the truth – I usually have a healthy appetite all the time – but my suddenly knotted stomach made it true enough. Was he going to throw me out here and now?

"You won't…" Henry growled.

"Relax. I just want to talk for a minute and then she can come back." Taking my elbow he steered me out into the hallway and through the faux Victorian door onto the porch.

Contrary to the sickly heat of the day before, the morning was pleasant - humid, but comfortable. The sunlight glittered brightly and a slight breeze played down the length of the porch, teasing the tips of my hair. I barely noticed. This was the second time Ryan Cable had touched me, and once again it felt as if a live wire had been applied to my skin. I was grateful when he released me. Though good-looking, he was too rough-hewn to be considered truly handsome – unlike the beautiful Charley – but there was an essential power emanating from him that made me shiver.

This wouldn't do! I had work to do, not let myself act like a star-struck teenager. There was too much at stake here.

"Yes, Mr. Cable?"

He stood looking at me for a long moment, tapping those masking aviator sunglasses against his palm. His gaze, though fairly neutral, almost blistered.

"I just want to remind you that you aren't to shock or startle Uncle Henry. He's very old and sick. Don't let him work too long, either. He's not as strong as he thinks he is."

"I'm not a slave driver, Mr. Cable, but I think you should be telling him instead of me. If there's one thing I've learned about Mr. Wolfe it's that trying to stop him is sort of like trying to stop a train with a feather."

For the first time since we had met Ryan Cable laughed. His face crinkled with genuine humor and in that moment he was incredibly handsome. "You have it in one, Mrs. Grayson. Just do what you can." Still chuckling, he turned and almost bumped into Charley.

How anyone could walk so silently across the noisy board porch in high-heeled cowboy boots I had no idea, but there he was.

"Miz Grayson." He nodded politely if curtly in my direction, then turned to Ryan. "Mr. Cable, can I talk to you a moment?"

I went back into the house. Petunia had cleared the table, which was fine with me. My knotted stomach would have rebelled at any more food. Henry Wolfe awaited me in the living room. The fire had not been lit, but the air conditioning made the room unpleasantly chilly after the balmy temperature outside.

"Well, Mrs. Grayson?" he asked in challenging tones.

"Well, Mr. Wolfe?" I answered in kind. "Are you ready to begin?"

He smiled. It was not a pleasant smile. "Let's get going."

I had had the presence of mind to bring my tablet down to breakfast; it now balanced on the arm of my chair. Normally I would have preferred a table, but at the moment that seemed superfluous. I sat and opened the keyboard case, then pulled up the list of questions. Most of the answers I already knew, but wanted to hear them in his own words.

"All right, Mr. Wolfe, you were born in a sharecropper's cabin…"

Chapter Four

"… AND THAT'S HOW I took over Kingman Paper Products," Henry said, a smug smile lifting the corners of his lips. "Good deal, that."

Dutifully I typed the information into my tablet, carefully keeping my face neutral. It was basically the same story as my research had given, but with an entirely different viewpoint. Judging from what the Kingman Paper CEO had said in several interviews and a careful perusal of a number of business articles at the time, Wolfe Industries had all but stolen the company and absorbed it. Oh, it was all legal, but still not nice, which seemed to be standard for Wolfe Industries. Business is business, but what rubbed me the wrong way was Henry's delight in having done it.

"All right," I said, saving the document and

closing my tablet, "that's enough for this morning. I'll go up and get some work done while you take a rest."

We had moved out onto the big shaded porch. In spite of the lazy ceiling fan above us it had become stiflingly hot, but Henry seemed to love it, so I had sweated in silence.

"What do you mean, rest?" Henry all but snarled. "Think this is a vacation? We've got a lot of work to do."

"None of which will get done if you wear yourself out. I'm under strict orders to keep our sessions short." I tried to sound impersonal.

"How's the book going?" Ryan asked, stepping out onto the porch and saving me from a blast of Henry's temper.

"Damned woman wants to quit for the morning. Says she's under orders to make me rest. I give the orders around here, so tell her she's wrong." He gave his grand-nephew an evil glare as Ryan sat down across the table.

"Now why would I want to do that?" He asked

with a tolerant smile. He had removed his suit jacket, loosened his collar and necktie, and rolled up his sleeves. My heart gave a funny little quiver. Some company was losing a bundle by not using him for a model. Two extremely attractive men in one house – it was nearly overwhelming.

Henry harrumphed. "What are you doing here this time of day? Don't you have an office to run?"

Remembering the orders he had given me that morning, I gave a sweet smile and said, "Probably checking up to make sure I don't work you too hard. I told you I wouldn't tire him out, Ryan."

We had not agreed to use first names; it just popped out.

Ryan laughed, but not as easily or as genuinely as he had the night before. "You don't hedge much, do you, Dianne? Yes, Uncle Henry, you know you get overtired easier than you will admit, so I talked to Mrs. Grayson and she agreed not to have long working hours."

"Bet your mother was involved in this, dratted hovering woman."

Vernita was Ryan's mother? It was all I could do to keep my mouth from falling open. That meant… I struggled to remember what I had learned about the family. That meant Ryan had to be the son from Vernita's first marriage, and Henry's sister's son's stepson.

"Of course. She cares for you, Uncle Henry. We all do. As for what I'm doing here, I've come home for lunch."

Was it lunchtime already? I had been vaguely conscious of an emptiness, but put it down to my truncated breakfast. Concentrating on Henry's story – and on keeping my mouth shut – I had completely let the time get away from me.

"For lunch?" Henry gave a sarcastic bray of laughter. "Since when do you do that?"

Ryan stood and reached for the handles of his uncle's wheelchair. "Since I have to protect you from a rampaging writer." His smile took away any sting the words might have had.

"More like the other way around," I said with an answering smile, saving the file and closing my tablet. I was only halfway kidding.

* * * * *

"So how is the book going?" Vernita asked, sitting at the end of the table, acting as gracious as a queen. Or, at least, as condescendingly gracious as one who has never met a queen might think.

Lunch was almost over. Having declined a positively luscious looking rice pudding for dessert, I sipped my iced tea, waiting for Henry to answer. When it became obvious that he wasn't going to say anything, I murmured, "Quite well, for the first day."

Actually, that wasn't altogether true. Henry had been quite forthcoming with information, it just wasn't the information I wanted. I had asked questions about his youth and young manhood, about his family – both when he had been a boy and after he had married. He had given almost monosyllabic answers and then gone on to expound about business and all the clever deals he had done. I could foresee that this could be a long process before I learned what I wanted to know.

"When will you begin writing?" Vernita asked,

her eyes bright with curiosity. "How long does it take to write a book?"

That was a question I hated, because it thoroughly exposed the ignorance of the questioner. I could hold forth for quite a long time about deadlines and inspiration and all the other claptrap that was used instead of how you just needed to put your buns in a chair and write for as long as it took, but it seemed much too much energy to expend when I had other things to think about.

"That depends on how long it takes me to get the information I need," I said. "Right now we're just in the information gathering stage."

Vernita looked disappointed, and I had the shivery premonition that she probably would like to write a book. Most people did, especially those who had no idea of the process or the effort needed.

"I hope Uncle Henry hasn't been working you too hard," Ryan said in a conversational tone.

"We haven't been working at all," Henry snapped. "Just talking. She asks more questions than you'd believe."

"And how else am I to get the information I need?"

He glared at me. "By listening to what I tell you, that's how. Don't need any tales about my private life."

"You hired me to write a book about you," I replied in reasonable tones. "That includes your private life."

"Not if I don't want it to."

"If all people wanted was to know about your business career, you could just cut and paste stories out of newspapers and business journals. Vernita could do that for you. You wouldn't need a writer."

Vernita gobbled as if I had shoved a pad and pen into her hands, while Ryan gave up trying to hold back a smile and roared.

"She's got you there, Uncle Henry."

Henry sent his grand-nephew a dirty look. "Whose side are you on, anyway?"

Still smiling, Ryan stood. "My own, of course. I'm going back to the office."

"Drive carefully," Vernita said.

"And you," Ryan added from the doorway, pointing his finger at Henry, "get some rest. I think this might be a fairly long project and you don't want to get tired out."

"That's a good idea," Vernita said. "You have to take care of your health, Uncle Henry."

Henry muttered something unintelligible, then glared at me. "I suppose you want me to rest, too."

I dabbed my lips and folded my napkin. Lunch had been delicious. I'd have to be careful here, or I'd grow out of my clothes in no time. "Actually, Mr. Wolfe, I don't care what you do. I am going up to my room and organize my notes, perhaps start working on a framework to present to you tomorrow."

"Tomorrow! You're not here for a vacation! We'll work this afternoon."

When he was angry Henry Wolfe was a force to be reckoned with, but I was determined not to let him get to me. I stood up. "This is far from a vacation, trust me. There is a lot more to writing a biography than just listening to stories or stringing words together. Now I'm going up to work."

Vernita smiled and patted Henry's hand. "See how things work out the way they're supposed to? You have a nice afternoon, Mrs. Grayson, and don't forget about drinks in the parlor at six-thirty."

Henry was answering her as I all but fled up the stairs. From the little that spilled out through the open door I was very glad I couldn't hear the rest.

I had just reached the landing when the door to my room closed.

Chapter Five

"I'M SORRY, MIZ Grayson," Charley said apologetically, stepping away from the door as if it were hot. "I was supposed to put that typing table in your room earlier this morning, but just couldn't get it up here until now."

I swallowed and tried to quieten my thudding heart. "That's all right. I've been downstairs all morning."

Nodding, he walked past me down the stairs.

I must admit it was with some trepidation I entered my room, but – with the exception of a simple table and a secretarial chair tucked in the corner – it appeared untouched. Of course I checked the huge wardrobe and the drawers, but nothing appeared to have been bothered, not that there was anything of interest in them. My laptop was the only possible weak link, and it was password protected. It was also in the drawer just as I had left it.

I really did need to get this morning's notes into some sort of order. Henry Wolfe was the kind of man who would demand to see what had been done so far. Plugging in both the computer and tablet I set to work, then once that chore was done I started putting the sparse information I had learned so far into a new file, one double-protected with its own password. There was little to record, but I had to keep reminding myself I had been here less than twenty-four hours.

That chore taken care of, I jumped on the internet and concentrated on research until a dull roaring forced its way into my consciousness. Turning to face the windows I was startled to see a world gone mad. The sky, a clear, robin's egg blue when I had sat down, was now a sullen and puffy grey-green. Beyond the lawn the guardian ring of trees whipped and danced as if possessed while branches and leaves flew through the air, carried on the shouting wind. The change was as terrifying as it was sudden. I had been working barely three hours yet the entire world was different.

Shutting down and unplugging both computer and tablet, I crept downstairs. The stairwell was almost as dark as night, the gaudily ornate pattern of the stained glass skylight merely a spattering of dark colors. The house seemed deserted. None of the night-light sconces had been turned on, and the house was filled with a murky semi-light that was uncomfortably like being under dirty water.

A small patch of slightly lighter dark glowed at the end of the corridor to the left of the stairwell, the one that went to the back of the house and presumably to the outside. I almost went that way, until two figures stepped into it. There was no question that it was Vernita and Charley, even though they were nothing but silhouettes. I almost spoke, but the words froze in my throat as he bent to kiss her. It was not a friendly kiss; even from this distance the sexual heat was almost palpable. Forcing my mouth shut, I stepped back into the shadows.

So the consciously gracious and condescending Vernita was getting a little lovin' from the hired man. Of course that was her business, but I couldn't help wondering if Ryan knew about his mother's activities with a man younger than he... and what he thought about it.

A small sound made me turn to the right, where a short corridor went off at a sharp angle. In the dim light there was the hint of a figure, little more than a moving shadow in the gloom, gliding away into the darkness.

Vernita and Charley were in the other hall. Henry was in a wheelchair. Ryan? Wouldn't he still be at work? Petunia? What would she be doing over here? Besides, what I had seen was much taller and more substantial than she.

Someone else? Who?

Curiosity had always been a failing of mine. Moving as quietly as I could I slid into the short hall. There were only two doors, so of course I picked the wrong one. It was a bathroom – plain but functional, and set up for handicapped use.

So the other door had to be Henry's office. I knocked and then, at his "Who is it?" let myself in.

He was alone, sitting in his wheelchair at a large and elegant desk. This was a big room, lined with bookshelves and furnished with overstuffed pieces reminiscent of an English gentlemen's club. Three tall French doors led out onto the porch and gave a good view of the garden beyond.

Could whoever it was have gotten out the French doors so quickly? Perhaps, but certainly not without Henry's seeing them. I began to feel uncomfortable.

"Mrs. Grayson," he said in neutral tones. "Are you done with your work?"

"For this afternoon, yes." I looked outside at the flailing plants.

"Want to sit down? I'll be done in a moment."

I sat on the big leather couch, but could not keep my eyes from staring out the French doors. "I don't think I've ever seen a sky like this," I said, trying to keep my voice steady. Storms had never been one of my favorite things. I liked a gentle rain, yes, but not this weird grey-green sky and howling wind.

"It's just a spring blow. Nothing to worry about." He was dismissive, but somehow that didn't make me feel any better.

Good grief, I thought in awe, *what would he worry about?*

"It's getting rough out there," Ryan said, stepping through the door. His hair had begun to curl slightly and sparkled with raindrops; a pattern of dark circles marked his shoulders. "Starting to rain."

"You're home early." Henry looked displeased.

"Wanted to get back before the storm got worse."

Henry harrumphed at that.

"Y'all through for the day?" Ryan flopped back easily in one of the leather club chairs.

The lights flickered and went out. Startled and terrified, I managed to both scream and jump in the few seconds before they came on again.

"Don't you like our weather, Mrs. Grayson?" Henry asked with a trace of contempt. I found myself wondering ungraciously just how he would act during one of our California earthquakes.

"It's all right," Ryan said with a smile in my direction. "Spring is our storm season. We've had worse than this. And don't worry about the lights. If the power goes off for more than ten minutes we have a generator that kicks in." He sounded almost proud.

"Oh my goodness, Ryan, I didn't know you'd come home so early." Vernita bounced through the door. "Charley said you were back."

Snidely I wondered how Charley knew that; he and Vernita had seemed preoccupied enough to miss almost anything.

Overhead there was a boom of thunder so intense it shook the double-paned windows. I jumped. Again.

"Mrs. Grayson doesn't like our weather," Henry said.

"Well, I can't blame her for that," Vernita replied tartly. "I don't either. Sometimes I swear we're just going to be blown clean away."

Henry snorted, but Ryan just laughed and said,

"Not likely, Mom. Don't worry, Mrs. Grayson. We have a storm cellar if we need it."

Somehow that didn't make me feel any better; neither did the fact that the heavens suddenly opened and rain poured down as if from a faucet.

"Thought y'all could use some iced tea," said Petunia, putting a silver tray on the desk. "Supper's going to be early. I want to get home before it gets bad."

Bad? It was going to get *worse*? I jumped again as more thunder exploded above us.

"Thank you, Petunia," Vernita said with a large dollop of graciousness toward Petunia's retreating back. "Call us when it's ready. Now, who wants tea?"

Obviously that was a rhetorical question, because she was already putting ice – from a sterling ice bucket, of course – and large sprigs of mint into the tall glasses.

"There's nothing to be afraid of, Mrs. Grayson," Ryan said, tugging his tie down. "Our storms are noisy, but they don't often turn into anything. *...full* *of sound and fury…*"

"… *signifying nothing…*" I finished the quote, then made the stupidest mistake of my life. My only defense is that the storm – and the situation – had unnerved me. "My mother said that a lot."

"Your mother told you about East Texas weather?" Henry asked in tones almost as sharp as the crackle of thunder above. A burst of lightning illuminated the world in a brilliant white light, for a millisecond obliterating everything.

"Yes…" I allowed myself to say, then shut my mouth in case something even more damning should slip out.

"Then did she tell you why she ran away from her home?" Henry brought his fist down on his desk so hard that it rivaled the boom of thunder outside. "Did she tell you why she left her family who had never done anything but love her and did everything that was good for her?"

Caution was obliterated and a lifetime's worth of frustration bubbled to the surface as I stared at the harsh face of Henry Wolfe.

My mother's father.

My grandfather.

Chapter Six

VERNITA GAVE A small shriek as the cut glass pitcher slipped from her hand to bounce on the polished floor, sending tea spraying. Miraculously it didn't break, but no one seemed to notice.

"Your mother? Stephanie was your mother?" she squeaked.

Ryan, I noticed, didn't appear to be surprised at all.

"What was good for her?" I shouted, too far gone to be cautious, which was probably good since the cat was now most definitely out of the bag. "That's a lie! You tried to use her as a puppet to forward your ambition!"

"I wanted what was best for her! Curse it, woman, if she'd played her cards right she could have been the First Lady of Texas, maybe even someday the First Lady of the United States! Instead she runs off with a high school dropout whose father was a drunk and his mother a whore. They came around here for years trying to get money out of me."

"You mean those horrible O'Malleys that used to live down near Dead Woman Creek?" Vernita asked in shrill tones of horror. "They were nothing but the worst kind of poor white trash!"

"My mother loved my father, and she didn't marry his mother or his father," I snapped. "He owned the best garage in the county and became a captain in the volunteer fire department. He even graduated from college." Though it had been almost a year I was suddenly overwhelmed with a crushing sense of loss. My eyes filled with tears and it was all I could do not to sob like a baby. "She was proud of him. I was too. You pushed her at a man she didn't like."

"Billy Don Prendergast is a good solid man from a good family."

"Billy Don Prendergast is a slimy, repulsive

weasel with delusions of grandeur and hands that went everywhere they shouldn't! Mother hated him."

Angry, Henry made a dismissive gesture. "He was just a boy."

"Weasels don't change."

"Why didn't you tell us who you were before?" Vernita asked with a fearful frown.

"I was hired to come write a book. Henry… Grandfather…" My voice dripped with sarcasm on the word, but I couldn't help it. "Why didn't you tell me you knew about our relationship?"

"Why should I? I knew you'd show up sometime, wanting to get in on the gravy train. I just wanted to do it on my terms."

That took my breath away. "You think I'm here because I want your money? That's horrible."

"Now let's just all cool our jets a little…" Ryan began, but both Henry and I ignored him, just as we were ignoring the worsening weather. The storm outside was nothing compared to the storm seething inside.

"You're here, aren't you?"

"You brought me here to write a book."

"But you didn't tell us who you were."

"I'll be gone as soon as I can pack," I said, standing.

"Now wait just a minute," Ryan said in a voice so authoritative even Henry turned to look. "There's a storm out there. We need to get this worked out, and once we do I'll drive you to the airport myself. When the weather clears."

"Don't worry, Ryan," Henry said in a horrid voice. "She won't leave until she figures out how much money she can get from me."

Curling my fingers into a tight fist, I had never felt more like physical violence in my life. "Mr. Wolfe, I did not come here to get any part of your fortune. I think our contract is now void, don't you agree? I'll return the advance you gave me, as well as reimburse you for my plane ticket, and pay for my room and board here so far, if you like. I'll even sign any legal paper you like giving up any right I might ever have to your money. I only want two things from you."

Henry gave a snide laugh. "I knew it. Sounds so altruistic, doesn't she, Ryan, but she does want something. I knew it."

Ryan's face was hard. "And what would those two things be, Dianne?"

"My mother's portrait, and her red spinel ring."

"You'd give up a fortune for a picture and a ring?" He sounded skeptical.

"Yes, I would." My anger vanished as memories washed over me. The ring had been my grandmother's. Mother had loved that ring, and whenever she talked about it she became melancholy and wistful. Sometimes I thought it was the only thing from her old home she missed. I hadn't known of the portrait's existence until last night, but I wanted it for me with a passion. "Have a paper written up any way you want cutting me out of your fortune and I'll sign it in exchange for the portrait and the ring."

"That's foolish," Ryan said. "You'd be a very rich woman."

"I don't care. I'm making decent money on my

own. I just want that picture and that ring."

Henry snorted. "Stupid woman. They lied to you. That man she married probably sold it, because your mother took that ring with her when she left."

* * * * *

The world swirled around me in a dizzying kaleidoscope of color and feelings, making me sick to my stomach. Could it be possible? Why? Had Daddy taken the ring and sold it? Had Mother lied to me?

The world righted and solidified once more. My father had been the most honorable man I had ever known, and my mother incapable of telling a lie. Her grief about her ring had been genuine.

"You are a horrible old man," I said, "and a damned liar." With that I ran out onto the porch. I had to get out of that room, quit breathing the same air as Henry Wolfe, and for once I didn't care what kind of storm was going on.

At least until I was outside. The wind almost pushed me against the house, and the raindrops, which were nearly as big as eggs, slammed against me like thrown pebbles. The porch was deep, but the roof was of little protection. Almost instantly I was soaking wet from the waist down and stumbling to keep my balance.

Strong arms wrapped around me and held me close. "You silly little fool," Ryan said into my ear. "People can die in this kind of storm. Let's go back inside."

I struggled against him, totally without result. His arms were like iron bands around me. "I will not go back in with that horrible old man!"

"All right, but we're both soaking. We'll go in through the parlor."

It was a struggle to walk against the wind even for the two of us, but once we had rounded the corner of the house the wind decreased a little, just enough to where we could stand erect. He didn't let go of me, though, and deep in my inmost thoughts I really didn't want him to. I had known Ryan Cable only a little more than a day, and already I was more physically attracted to him than I had ever been to the man I had cared enough about to marry.

Fumbling in his pocket while he held me tightly with one arm, Ryan pulled out a bunch of keys and unlocked one set of French doors, then pulled me into the living room. He released me only long enough to wrestle the doors shut and locked against the wind, then put his arm back around my shoulders. In truth, I was glad of it. Although the air conditioning was still on, it was warmer than the icy rain outside, but not enough to keep away my shivers and chattering teeth.

"You're freezing. Come on, let's get you upstairs."

"Just long enough to pack," I said, as defiantly as I could while keeping my tongue from being bitten. "Then I want to leave."

He steered me inexorably toward the stairs. "No one's going anywhere for a while, not in weather like this. Right now you need a hot bath to get you warmed up."

Part of me rebelled against the thought of staying in this house one minute longer, but my practical side could appreciate the logic of this – and his mention of a hot bath brought up sensual images that even I found shocking. No, the sooner I was away from Wolfe House and all it stood for the happier I would be.

But not without my mother's picture and her ring!

We stopped at the door to my room, which Ryan opened like a gentleman. "Now you go soak in a hot tub and warm up, then get dressed. I'll come and fetch you for supper."

"I'll have my meal in my – ouch! – room," I said imperiously, though it is hard to be imperious when your chattering teeth bite a fair sized chunk of your tongue.

He smiled, and my knees went weak. "You aren't such a coward. I'll be back up to get you in about forty-five minutes." Then he gently pushed me inside and pulled the door closed behind me.

I must have stood for a full minute staring at the closed door and hating the fact that he was right. I have never been a coward; neither of my parents would have allowed it. *'We face things,'* Daddy had said, *'whether we want to or not, and that makes us stronger.'*

Henry Wolfe would not beat me, in either sense of the word.

He wouldn't dare.

Chapter Seven

RYAN'S SUGGESTION OF a hot bath was wonderful; I lay in the tub for at least half an hour, until I was pink and tingly all over, before dressing in the same jeans and blazer I had worn yesterday. This time, though, I chose a simple t-shirt instead of my pretty blouse. This was the way I dressed, doggone it, and it didn't make any difference if Henry Wolfe didn't like women in pants or not. Besides, I hadn't brought any skirts with me.

I didn't wait for Ryan to come escort me down. Outside the storm still went on, but not as badly as before. This time the stairwell sconces were on and pushed back the storm-blackness a little, though the rain still rattled threateningly on the stained-glass roof. At this rate it would probably continue all night, and Heaven only knew what the roads between here and the Longview airport would be like tomorrow. It was very possible that I could be stuck here for several days, so might as well make the best of it. I went down the stairs with as much confidence as I had ever had. Henry Wolfe might be a lying old man with a black heart and a shriveled soul, but I was not going to cringe in front of him. My parents wouldn't have allowed it, and neither would I.

Light spilled out from the open living room door, so I went in there, braced for the worst. A small fire was lit, and Henry sat beside it in his wheelchair, blanket across his lap and a drink in his hand. His eyes were as cold as the icy rain had been. I met his stare straight on for a full three seconds before looking over toward Ryan, who was lounging on one of the matching loveseats.

Now he was wearing worn jeans and a lightweight sweater – and I'll admit it, looking absolutely delicious. He unfolded from the loveseat and walked to the bar. "What can I get you to drink, Dianne?"

"Can I have a glass of white wine, please?" I sat on the other loveseat, consciously choosing to be directly across from Henry.

He sniffed. "A Californian's idea of a drink."

"You've been known to like a touch of the grape too, Uncle Henry."

"With dinner, yes. It's civilized. But not a drink. Not for a Texan, at least."

Mean spiritedly I wished I had ordered something really esoteric, like vermouth or Campari, but took the exquisite crystal glass Ryan extended and sipped. I wasn't an expert, but there was no question this wine was good. Very good. Had my mother grown up with this kind of quality, this kind of luxury, and walked away without a qualm to marry my father? I had always known they had a special kind of love, but this just underscored how very special it had been.

"Will it do?" Ryan asked, and I realized it was for the second time.

"Yes – it's quite good. Sorry. I was just thinking about my mother growing up here and – " I added only halfway spitefully " – how much she loved my father."

Henry frowned and rumbled deep in his throat, but said nothing.

"Oh!" Vernita bumbled into the room, almost tripping over her own feet as she saw me. "I didn't know you were here."

"I remember Petunia said dinner would be early," I said smoothly. "So I came on down."

"Well, we'd all better go on in. Y'all can bring your drinks," she said with a bright smile, one so false that I wondered what would have happened had I not joined the family. A tray in my room? Anything?

Obediently we followed her into the dining room, where Petunia was putting out bowls of food.

"After all, we don't want to keep Petunia," Vernita said graciously. "She wants to go home as quickly as she cleans up after dinner."

Petunia was crazy, I decided, glancing out the French doors. In the deepening light it was obvious the storm still blasted on, though considerably less than before. It would probably rain all night.

Henry growled. As a writer I knew it was wrong to use animalistic attributions to describe human sounds, but sometimes it was the only thing that fit. Someone with their eyes closed would swear that an uncertain-tempered mastiff had wandered into the room.

"Storm might get worse later. Petunia, go home when you've finished serving. Vernita can clean up the kitchen when we finish."

Petunia muttered a thanks and actually looked happy. By contrast, Vernita did not. A look of shock passed over her face, followed by a distinctly unhappy expression.

"Won't you, Vernita?" Henry asked.

Her face calm as if the previous expression had never existed, Vernita nodded. "Of course, Uncle Henry. I'd be right proud to. I think I can still find my way around a kitchen."

"Some okra, Uncle Henry?" Ryan asked, extending a bowl.

For a few minutes we concentrated on filling our

plates.

Vernita ostentatiously took the first 'hostess' bite, before which no one was supposed to eat.. "I swear, Petunia has surpassed herself. This squash is superb."

"She is indeed a good cook," I said.

"Your mother used to say the same thing," Henry said provocatively. He watched me closely from under his shaggy brows.

"Petunia has been with you a long time then." I tried to keep my voice level, but my stomach was twisting.

"Your mother never told you about her." Now it was obvious he was being deliberate in his provocation.

"Uncle Henry…" Ryan said in tones of caution, but Henry ignored them, his full attention focused on me.

"No. She never mentioned anything about her former home, other than the spinel ring."

Henry growled again. It was a sound that would have sent that uncertain-tempered mastiff running.

"I asked her a couple of times growing up, but she wouldn't say much. I quit asking when I saw how much it hurt her."

"Hurt her?" An indefinable emotion flickered briefly in his eyes so quickly it might not have been before his expression turned stony once more. "She's the one who chose to live in a crackerbox house with the son of a bum."

"My father was an honorable and respected man…" I began, then stopped, my fork hanging in mid-air. Our family home had been modest but nice, yet to someone who lived in a mansion like this it could have been considered a 'crackerbox.' "You knew," I breathed. "You knew where we were."

This time his growl was a little less assured. "Of course I did."

"So you knew there was nothing bad about my father, how much he had achieved, how much he was respected. Then you knew about me, and you knew when they died, and you didn't even call. You didn't even care that I might have been left alone, that I might have needed someone."

91

He said nothing. His face looked so hard it could have been carved from granite.

"Uncle Henry made sure that you had friends around you and that you needed for nothing," Ryan said, but he sounded hesitant, as if embarrassed.

"I don't need anything from him," I snapped. "But for some strange reason my mother loved him. I cannot believe he knew where she was for years and made no effort to contact her!" I glared at Henry, who glared right back at me.

"She is the one who left," he said in a low voice. "She knew she could come home any time she asked. All those years and never a word from her. Not one!"

"Liar!" I smacked the table with my fist, so hard that it made the china jump. "That is a lie! She wrote you at least three times I can remember, and cried for days at a time when each letter was returned marked 'Refused.'"

He stared at me for a moment, a strange expression on his face. Someone charitable might have called it confusion, but I thought it was more hatred. "Then she was acting, because she never sent a letter. Not one…"

Had it been anyone but Henry Wolfe, had he been doing anything but lying about my mother, I might have thought he was emotionally touched.

But this *was* Henry Wolfe, and I had seen those 'Refused' letters returned from here myself, so all it meant was that he was a very good actor.

"Dianne – " Ryan began, but his mother interrupted.

"Now come, y'all," Vernita said uneasily, looking from one of us to the other, "this is dinner. We should be civilized. I won't have any more such kind of talk, hear?"

It was a mild reproof, but enough. I don't know why Henry obeyed so meekly. He was completely capable of annihilating anyone with whom he disagreed, but he contented himself with a glare at me. I glared back, but held all the probably unwise things that danced on my tongue. In spite of my impetuous words earlier I wanted to stay until I got some answers – as well as the portrait and the ring –

and I didn't intend to be precipitately thrown out.

"Have you made any progress on the book?" Ryan asked, after a long period of silence. Vernita rose and began to clear the table.

"It's too early to start on the book itself. There's a lot more research needed."

Henry rumbled again, this time sounding more like a sleeping volcano. "So you're going to stay and write?" He made it sound like an accusation.

"We have a contract," I returned, deliberately keeping my tone businesslike. "Unless you want to buy it off."

For a microsecond his eyes twinkled. "So you're a good businesswoman. Maybe there is something of the Wolfes in you after all."

"I hope not," I said with a sweet smile. "I'm an O'Malley."

Chapter Eight

ON THE OTHER hand, maybe I was not wholly O'Malley. Vernita bustled in with a tray of dessert service pieces and a large casserole dish. The aroma alone almost brought tears to my eyes.

"It looks like Petunia left us a good dessert." She busied herself with serving and passing out heaping bowls. Henry, of course, got the first dish.

I looked at the stuff, then took a cautious bite. As I had thought, it was a deliciously spicy raisin bread pudding, topped with a tangy brandy-vanilla hard sauce. My eyes filled and I batted away the tears.

"Don't you like it?" Ryan asked.

I shook my head. "This was my mother's favorite dessert. She made it often."

"Stephanie always liked this," Henry said in a

suspiciously soft voice.

"Did Petunia work here when my mother was here?" I hadn't intended to expose myself so openly, but the words just came out.

"Petunia has worked here since Uncle Henry bought the house," Ryan said.

"And has been taking advantage ever since." Vernita's tone was tart. "I mean, look. She wanted to go home early because of the weather – leaving me with cleaning up the kitchen, I might add – "

"You've cleaned a kitchen before, Mom," Ryan said in an impossibly light tone, but it wasn't enough to stop her.

"Yes, I have, but that doesn't give Petunia the right to shift her job off onto me. Because of the weather, my foot! She knew the weather would break. I mean, just look at that."

I glanced out the French doors to a startling sight. The rain had ceased to nothing but a light pitter-patter as quickly as if some celestial faucet had been turned off. The clouds were still there, but they had lightened to a pale grey and seemed to be pulling back from the earth as they shredded. Sunlight poured through here and there like liquid gold.

"Humph," Henry snorted. "The devil's beating his wife again." He turned to me. "That means – "

"That there's sunshine and rain at the same time. Yes, I know. Mother used to tell me that."

"Texas weather," Ryan said quickly, scooping up the last of his pudding. "If you don't like it, just wait a couple of minutes."

"We say that in California, too," I said, mesmerized by the transformation outside. We said that too, but our weather didn't change so quickly or so dramatically.

"And you know it could just as easily have gotten worse," Henry said to Vernita, his voice ostentatiously neutral. "Besides, Petunia deserves an occasional night off."

"She gets all of Saturday and Wednesday night too…" Vernita began, but Henry froze her with a glare.

"That is enough, Vernita. I'm tired of your

complaining."

"Of course, Uncle Henry. I'm sorry." Vernita's tone was meek and her lip trembled.

What a dishrag she was! I tried to keep the contempt I felt from showing in my face. Henry treated her like a servant. No, that wasn't quite true; any servant worth his salt would leave the first time he pulled a stunt like that, and servants were hard to find.

"If y'all are finished now," Vernita said, standing but being very careful that Henry didn't see her face. "I'll clear this away and go start on the kitchen."

I almost volunteered to help, but caught myself in time. I wasn't the daughter of the house, and I wasn't an honored guest. I was here to work on a book – if Henry and I decided we were going to continue the project. That was not a given, not by me at least.

Henry decided the matter, as he was wont to decide everything. "Dianne, push me into the parlor. We need to talk."

"I'll take you, Uncle Henry," Ryan said, standing, but Henry waved him away.

"No, I want Dianne. We need to talk. You go help your mother."

A flash of an unrecognizable emotion flickered over his face, but Ryan obediently picked up the stack of dirty plates and followed his mother to the kitchen. I grabbed the handles of Henry's wheelchair and pushed him into the parlor. Parking the chair where it had been earlier I sat in the facing chair. Now that the rain and thunder were gone, a thick silence filled the room, a silence I would not be the first to break.

As the minutes mounted it seemed we might sit like that until we mummified, but finally Henry cleared his throat and spoke.

"Are you planning to stay and finish the book?"

"As for the book, I don't know," I replied as neutrally as possible. "That depends on you. As for staying here, I fully intend to until I get my mother's portrait and her ring."

"I told you she took the ring with her."

"And I told you she never had it. She mourned for that ring all her life."

"Then that bum she married took it and sold it."

Anger flared in me both hot and fast, but I clenched my jaw and refused to move or speak until I could do so calmly. "That isn't true and you know it. Apparently you have watched us all these years, so you know what kind of a man my father was. He wouldn't take anything that wasn't his."

"When they left they didn't have anything. He could have – "

"No, he wouldn't," I interrupted sharply. "The essentials of a person don't change, and he was a good man."

"A good man doesn't encourage a woman he is supposed to love to run away with him. A good man doesn't take her away from a good and comfortable life."

"And he didn't. Mother told me many times how she almost had to force him to run away with her. You see, she was going whether or not he went with her. There was no way she'd stay with what was going on."

Henry was good at controlling his features, but not that good. A look of surprise flashed over his face. "She? Stephanie? Why? If there was something wrong, why didn't she come to me? I would have taken care of it."

"You were it," I said brutally, then regretted it. "You were forcing her to marry Billy Don Prendergast."

"I was not!"

"You were planning her wedding to him. She couldn't stand to be in the same room with him and you were pushing her to marry him. How could you?"

His face crumbled and suddenly he looked a thousand years old. "Go away and leave me alone. Send Ryan to me."

Set in the back of the house and very easy to find, the kitchen at Wolfe House was in keeping with the rest of the place – impeccably maintained and stylish for its time. It was also huge, with room for both a large island and a breakfast table. I felt a rush of pure envy, for my apartment kitchen was barely big enough to turn around in, and the kitchen in my parents' house had scarcely been larger.

"Ryan? Henry wants you. He's in the parlor."

Without a word Ryan put down the towel and the plate he had been drying. More for want of something to do with my hands than from any real desire to help I picked up the plate and the towel.

"Be careful with those," Vernita commented in a neutral voice.

Not far from the sink the dishwasher hummed quietly. I dried the plate with care and then put it on a stack of its fellows before picking up another.

"These wouldn't fit in the dishwasher?"

Vernita gave me a glance that could have withered a houseplant. "You don't put fine china or sterling in a dishwasher. Didn't your mother teach you that?" she said in tones that made it clear I was a barbarian.

"No, we didn't have fine china or sterling," I returned easily. My status in her mind – already quite low – obviously sank even further.

We worked through the rest of the china in silence, then Vernita drained the soapy side of the sink and refilled it, finally adding the heavy silver flatware.

"Your mother shouldn't have hurt her father so," she said at last, eyes firmly fixed on the sink.

I grabbed some of the silver she had washed and rinsed and began polishing every piece with care. If I scratched one this group was probably capable of execution!

"Her father shouldn't have tried to force her into marriage with a man she found abhorrent. Her father should have responded when she reached out to him."

"He wasn't forcing her – just trying to make her see what a good match it would be. Billy Don comes from one of the finest families in this part of the country. Wealthy, too. She had no call to say the bad things about him she did. He was just a boy, after all, and they pull all kinds of stupid pranks."

Mother had told me about some of the things Billy Don had done. Strange how some people could dismiss sexual assault and attempted rape as a boy's stupid pranks.

"You know Uncle Henry wrote you out of the will," she said, and though she tried there was no disguising the faint note of triumph in her voice.

"That's not surprising." I had expected no less.

"You aren't going to get him to change his mind."

"I'm not going to try," I began, prepared to say again all I wanted was the portrait and the ring, but we were interrupted.

"Miz Wolfe?" The back door opened and Charley stepped in. He might have been speaking to Vernita, but his attention was on me. "I thought you'd like to know there's been some flooding in the tomato garden."

Frowning, Vernita rinsed her hands and ran outside, muttering something about how she hoped the plants could be saved. I didn't see how much of anything could not be flooded after the downpour, but maybe they built things differently here in Texas. By the time I had finished drying all the silverware she hadn't come back, so I went ahead and finished what was left, then rinsed and dried them, leaving everything on the counter.

Ryan came back in just as I had finished and was hanging the dish towel to dry. "What's going on? Where's Mom?"

"Charley came and got her. Something about the tomatoes flooding."

He frowned briefly; maybe he really liked tomatoes. "You didn't have to do any of this."

"I know."

"Come on. We need to talk." Taking my arm, he steered me through the house to the parlor, then opened the French doors to the porch. "I think the chairs are dry enough."

They were. We sat on opposite sides of the little table. It was beautiful after the rain. The low sun had sunk just to the level of the surrounding treetops and poured a lacy light over the various greens of the lawn and surrounding trees, while the sky, now nearly innocent of clouds, was an intense blue. A fresh breeze, still bearing the scent of rain, breathed past us, making it almost cool.

"This is lovely," I said after a while, when it became obvious that in spite of his announcement he wasn't going to say anything.

"It is, especially after a rain."

"What did you want to talk to me about?"

He sighed. Leaning forward, hands clasped and elbows on knees, he looked up at me. "You know Uncle Henry wrote your mother and you out of his will years ago."

"Yes. Your mother told me."

He looked startled, but his voice was still gentle. "I've been trying to get him to correct that, but…"

"Well, please don't. I don't want anything from him. Except…"

"Except the portrait and the ring."

"Yes."

"That's not very smart."

"Perhaps not. But that's the way it is." I'll admit it was harder and harder to say that. The siren thoughts of a lot of money could corrupt anyone. Still, it was Henry's money, and I didn't want money or much of anything else from a man who could cut his only child so completely out of his life.

"Well, I'm sure we can come to some sort of agreement about the portrait," he said slowly, "but the ring – it hasn't been seen around here since the night your mother left."

So he was sticking to the party line. I took a quick intake of breath, and when I answered was careful to be sure that my voice was as civilized and passionless as his. "She didn't take it with her. I'll guarantee that. She grieved for it until she died."

"I know you don't want to consider it, but is it possible that your father – ?"

"No. She didn't take it with her because it was upstairs in her room in her jewel box. She hadn't worn it that night. When she left after a terrible fight with her father she had just come into the house. She didn't even go back upstairs – just walked out of the house. All she had was her purse."

Ryan was sitting straight up now, looking at me as if wondering could I be believed. "It wasn't a planned elopement?"

"No. They had to sneak out for dates… Henry hated Daddy so he had a fit when he found out she'd been seeing him. Henry," I added bitterly, "had his own plans. He wanted to be the father-in-law of the governor and believed Billy Don would make it."

"He still might," Ryan admitted sourly. "He's quite a wheel in politics around here. And your mom just left?"

"Henry was waiting for her when she came in. Daddy had just brought her home. He stood in the shadows on the drive until she got into the house. He'd started walking home when she went past him, running. He tried to make her go back, but she wouldn't hear of it. Said she'd go whether or not he approved. He went with her – to keep her out of trouble, he said – and they were together the rest of their lives." I stopped, surprised by the catch in my voice. A dribblet of tears formed in my eyes, but I blinked them back vigorously. I hadn't cried much since their deaths; if they had had to go, it seemed a blessing that they – who had never been separated for more than a few days – should have gone together.

"Your father sounds like a remarkable man."

"He was. That's why it makes me so furious that Henry is being such a bastard about it all." I seldom used even the mildest of curse words, but this time it seemed appropriate. My only regret was that Henry wasn't there to hear it.

"Henry suffered too, you know. He loved your mom. She was all he had left after his wife died."

"But he would sell her into a miserable marriage."

"He thought he was doing the best for her. She was a frivolous kind of girl back then."

I made a sound low in my throat, stopping when I realized it was remarkably like Henry growling. "You knew my mother?"

He nodded. "We came here right after my stepfather died. I was probably four or so, but I remember her well. I thought she was a fairy princess. So beautiful, and always so prettily dressed... Yes," he added with a soft laugh, "little boys notice that sort of thing. She was always nice to me, too. Mom and I had had a hard time of it – bad enough that after Uncle Robert died we sometimes went hungry. She didn't know how to do much of anything except keep house, you see, so when Uncle Henry offered her a job here it was like a gift from Heaven."

I looked at him. Tall, handsome, successful, self-assured… it was hard to picture him as a small boy who sometimes went hungry.

"So Vernita knew my mother too."

"Sure."

"Were they friends?"

Ryan looked out over the rain-soaked lawn. I couldn't see his face. "Not really, but they got along well enough."

"Who is Henry's heir?" I asked, surprising myself as much as him.

Looking me straight in the eye, he said "I am."

Chapter Nine

RYAN SHRUGGED, BUT his expression remained steady. "There is a settlement for Petunia and my mother, of course, and something for Charley and Dave, the plant manager, plus a few others and a couple of charities, but I'm the major recipient."

"Makes sense," I said easily. "You have been here most of your life and apparently you run the company – companies? – so it looks to me like you've earned it."

"You aren't upset?"

"Why would I be?" I shrugged and looked out over the clearing that surrounded the house. The sun had sunk well below the treetops and while the sky was still a brilliant blue barely stained with the colors of sunset the cup formed by the surrounding trees was filling with deepening shadows that looked like dirty water. "Yes, it would be wonderful to be filthy rich, but Henry doesn't owe me anything. I told him that I don't want his fortune and I mean it."

"You are a remarkable woman, you know that?" he asked, an admiring light in his eyes, then suddenly slapped his arm. "Damn! The mosquitoes are coming out. Dusk is the worst time for them, you know."

"No, I didn't." I slapped at my own arm, killing one almost as big as a hummingbird and splattering blood over a fair patch of skin. "Good grief, look at that!"

Ryan stood and extended his hand. "Come on, let's go inside. You aren't used to our Texas-sized bugs."

I took his hand and stood, trying to ignore that persistent tingle which happened every time we touched. He helped me to my feet, and I couldn't help but wonder what it would be like if he kept pulling me right into his arms and kissed me... The possibilities made me giddy.

Okay, I thought, *this is silly*. I only met him

twenty-four hours ago! Still logic had a hard time standing up against pure animal attraction. Worse was that apparently he wasn't feeling the same vibe, for nothing could have been more correct than his releasing my hand, opening the door into the parlor and ushering me in.

After the brilliant sky outside the unlit parlor was shadowy, as was the darkened stairwell beyond. There was enough light, though, for me to see an unidentifiable figure skittering away into the darkness.

* * * * *

I slept well that night for two reasons. One was I stayed up late over my computer, inputting everything I had heard or noticed since coming here, then added everything I could remember from the little my mother had mentioned of her home and family; it was a disappointingly small amount. The second was the chair I had wedged under the knob of the hall door. If there were any footsteps outside my door that night I didn't hear them.

I awoke surprisingly refreshed and, after a

luxurious hot shower, dressed in jeans, t-shirt and a loose cotton shirt over it in lieu of a sweater. Who would have thought I'd need a sweater in Texas? I certainly hadn't. Already the house was uncomfortably chilly. These Texans and their air conditioning!

Breakfast produced a surprise. It sat waiting for me at the table.

"Hi," the surprise said, rising and extending his hand. "I'm Dave Mondel."

"How do you do?" Bemused, I took his hand. What was it about Texas that produced such good-looking men? Charley, Ryan and even Henry, who must have been a looker when he was young... Now there was Dave, so tall and rangy that he looked as if he had just walked in from a rodeo in spite of the fact he wore a very citified suit.

"Dave is our general manager," Henry said, putting down his coffee cup. "I knew you wanted to talk to him, so I asked him over."

So Henry was going ahead on the book. I might as well too, as I had no intention of leaving until I got the two things I wanted. Then I planned never to see anyone or anything in this part of the country again.

Reluctantly reclaiming my hand, I sat just as Petunia put a brimming plate in front of me. I instantly realized that it was *huevos rancheros* – tortillas topped with refried beans, fried eggs, crumbled white cheese, *pico de gallo* and a healthy serving of salsa – but I had never seen them done quite so exuberantly. There was more food on that plate than I usually ate in an entire day back home.

"What? Don't you like them?" Henry asked, misinterpreting my expression.

"I love *huevos rancheros*. Mother made them all the time since they were Daddy's favorite. I'm just not accustomed to such large servings."

Henry's face tightened, but I couldn't tell if it were because I mentioned my parents or if he read an implied criticism into my comment.

"Breakfast is the most important meal of the day," Dave said, turning his attention back to his plate, which appeared to hold a bigger serving than mine. "Especially when the sainted Petunia cooks it."

Petunia had been pouring coffee; she didn't stop, but chuckled a little. "You go on, Mr. Dave." It was the first time she had not appeared to be a robot. She was even smiling when she left the room.

"Petunia!" Ryan bellowed more than loud enough to be heard in the kitchen as he came into the room and took his chair. He was dressed for the office and carried a thick file folder which he handed to Dave. "I looked over these projections and made a few notes. Good job."

Petunia appeared at a run, a loaded plate for Ryan in her hands. He beamed and nodded appreciatively; apparently he loved *huevos rancheros* too.

"That include the logging rights on the Spinks place?" Henry asked, then at Ryan's nod smiled almost carnivorously. "Good. I told old Marshall Spinks I'd get his lumber someday. Old bastard told me I never would."

"Marshall Spinks has been dead for nearly

twenty years," Ryan said mildly.

"Doesn't matter," Henry harrumphed. "I still got the lumber."

"So you're doing a book on Henry," Dave said to me. "He said you wanted to talk to me."

I temporized. "We're still seeing if we can work together, but I would like to talk to you."

"I wondered what had brought you here at this hour." Ryan took a big gulp of coffee. "Judy doesn't usually let you out of the house so early."

Dave flushed. "Now, Ryan, next you'll be saying that I'm henpecked. Actually, Mrs, O'Malley, my wife is the sweetest little woman you'd ever want to meet."

There was a twinkle in Ryan's eye. The sneaky so-and-so had been letting me know Mr. Mondel was married.

"I'm sure she is, Mr. Mondel. Now - when can we talk?"

"Why, right now," said Henry. "Why do you think I had him come over here when he should be at the office? Soon as you're finished eating we can all go in my office and you can ask whatever you want to know."

What? I choked on my *huevos rancheros*, the spicy salsa and *pico de gallo* going down the wrong way and searing my lungs. I gasped for breath; instantly both Dave Mondel and Ryan were beside me, holding me and pounding vigorously on my back. It was all I could do to get breath enough to tell them to stop.

"Fool Petunia for giving you that hot salsa!"

"Really, Henry!" I wheezed. "This isn't hot at all. We do have hot sauce in California, you know," I couldn't help adding. "I just swallowed wrong."

"Here." Ryan pressed a water glass into my hand and I drank thirstily. It really didn't help the burning that much, but at least I could breathe again.

"Thanks. No, Henry, it wasn't the salsa." I took a deep breath. We were going to have to set some boundaries here. "It was you. You actually intend to sit in on my interview with Mr. Mondel?"

"Call me Dave," he said somewhat uncomfortably but no one listened.

"Of course I do. It's my book."

"And I'm writing it. I never allow anyone to sit in on my interviews. Period."

The tension crackled in the air as if there were another thunderstorm brewing in spite of the fact it was bright and sunny outside.

Ryan chuckled. "I think I'd better get on down to the mill. It'll be safer there. Coming, Dave?"

He looked as if he would like nothing better, but Dave shook his head. "Nope. Rest of the week is full, so if Mrs. O'Malley wants to talk to me, it has to be this morning."

I got my way in the end, but the results weren't worth the effort. In spite of the glaring sun and a stiff breeze Dave Mondel and I settled in the shade of the porch and he very punctiliously answered every question I put to him. The fact that his answers might as well have been memorized from a script written by Henry himself didn't surprise me; Henry could have been sitting there beside us pulling Dave's strings like a marionette. It made me angry. Dave made Henry sound two short steps down from a saint, a virtuous man of the highest morals and ethics, a kindly and benevolent employer.

Even if I were inclined to believe such over-the-top praise, it was common knowledge people didn't build an empire and a fortune like Henry's by being kindly and benevolent. After half an hour I ended the charade and – with a great deal of politeness and hand-shaking on both sides – sent Dave back to work.

"Well?" Henry asked, wheeling himself out from his office as the front door closed. "What did Dave say about me?"

"Probably just what you told him to say. And just what I expected."

His face darkened, but his voice stayed pleasant. "Well, let's get back to it. I've dug out some old files you might want to look at."

"This afternoon. I want to type up these notes while they're fresh in my mind."

I had expected some resistance, but he merely shrugged and wheeled himself back into his office. It was true, I did need to type up the notes, but I didn't go upstairs. The notes could wait for a while. Instead, I walked down the hall to the kitchen.

Petunia stood at the big central worktable, mixing what I hoped was lunch, because it smelled delicious.

"Can I get you something, Mrs. O'Malley?" she asked civilly, but her eyes were sharp and gauging.

"No, thank you, Petunia, but I would like to talk to you if I may."

"For that book about Mr. Henry?"

I shook my head. "No, not really. What I really wanted to know was if you knew my mother."

A fleeting look of tenderness flashed over her features while the absence of any surprise or confusion confirmed that everyone around here now knew who I was.

"Of course I did. I went to work for Miss Sarah – your grandmother – first week she and Mr. Henry were married, back when they lived in that little house out toward the mill. Night your mother was born I was there all night, waiting for Mr. Henry to get home from the hospital and tell me how things had gone…" Her face softened with the memory. Her hands dropped to the table, uncharacteristically still.

"Your mother was a healthy baby, but her coming was awful hard on your grandmother. That's why your mother was an only child. Mr. Henry wouldn't have had anything happen to your grandmother, not for the world. In fact, he bought this house for her when she was still in the hospital recuperating." Her wrinkled face took on a glow of happy memory. "I remember when he came back to the house after he first saw the place. Asked me to go look at it with him and tell him if I thought she'd like it. Place was a wreck then; it took him almost four months to get it good enough for her."

"Sarah was in the hospital that long?"

"No, only about three weeks, but he ordered everyone not to tell her anything about it. I helped with the paint choices and such, though Mr. Henry had the final say." There was a ring of pride in her voice. "Then one day when the house was ready they went for a drive – left your mother home with me –

and he took her to the house. You never saw a happier woman than Miss Sarah! She never expected such a thing, especially after he done bought her that big red ring when Miss Stephanie was born." A dark shadow passed over her expression.

"My mother didn't take that ring with her, Petunia. She left it here."

"Then that man she went away with must have stole and sold it."

"No, the ring stayed here." I was getting tired of saying that. "Tell me about my grandmother."

For a moment it seemed as if she were going to clam up, but after a minute she took up a spoon and began to work again. "Miss Sarah was a Goodman from Dallas. One of the most beautiful women you'd ever want to see. You look a little like her, like your mama did, but neither one of you got a patch on her. She went to Baylor, down in Waco, but she met a friend of Mr. Henry's at some party and they got along real well. She came down here to visit him, but then he introduced her to Mr. Henry, and that was all she wrote! They were married inside of three months, and never were two people happier."

"When did she die?" I knew the date, but precious little else. Mother had always teared up when talking about her mother, so I had learned not to ask.

"When your mother was about ten. Miss Sarah'd gone into Longview to do some shopping. Your mother was in school. There was a wreck – a lumber truck going too fast. Miss Sarah's car was hit. She lived, but not for long – just enough for Mr. Henry and your mother to get to the hospital for a last goodbye. Miss Stephanie told me that her mother gave her that ring then, right off her finger, just before she died."

No wonder Mother had mourned for that ring.

"That's tragic, for everyone."

"Especially for Mr. Henry, after he was arrested."

"Arrested? For what?"

"For beating that truck driver near to death. The man deserved it, of course. Law had no call to interfere."

I stared. Was that an example of Texas justice? "Was Henry put in prison?"

"They kept him in jail for a while – until his lawyers could get him out. One of the Goodman cousins came down to look after Miss Stephanie – as if I couldn't have done that all right and proper! – and she ended up staying until she died. Nasty old woman she was, too, but after Mr. Henry got out he let her stay – said he didn't want any more upset for Miss Stephanie. Would have been better had he paid more attention to the girl, but after Miss Sarah died he seemed to live at the office. Like he couldn't bear to be here without her."

Poor Mother. Losing her mother and pretty much her father all at once. "When did Vernita come?"

"Not long after old Miss Goodman passed on – your mama was about fifteen or sixteen then."

"Where is Vernita? I haven't seen her this morning."

Petunia snorted as impressively as Henry ever did. "She's upstairs in bed with another one of her sick headaches."

So there really was no love lost between Petunia and Vernita. "Ryan said he remembered my mother."

"He should. They lived together in this house for over a year. He was a cute little boy, and she was real sweet to him, too, even when his mama was doing her darnedest to catch Mr. Henry's eye."

"Vernita was in love with Henry?"

"In love with his money'd be more like it," Petunia said in bald honesty. "Took her forever to realize that Miss Sarah was the only woman for him. But – " here she shrugged philosophically " – she quietened down and has done a right fair job as housekeeper."

"What about Ryan?"

"He's a good man. Was a good boy, too, better than one could expect from such a meachin' useless mother and a father that was no better than a gangster. Don't know what would have become of him if his mama hadn't married Mr. Henry's nephew. He's grown up right proud, Ryan has, and is a real help to Mr. Henry, both here and at the office. He deserves what he gets."

"I know he's my grandfather's heir," I said. "And that's fine with me."

She eyed me for a long few seconds, then turned her head back to her cooking. "It was God's blessing he was here for Mr. Henry, or we'd have lost him for sure."

"What do you mean, Petunia?"

"Well, I'm not one for gossip, but about a year ago Mr. Henry had a long run of bad luck. He took a fall down the stairs – wasn't using the elevator then. It had been put in for Miss Sarah at the beginning, but she didn't use it more than a time or two. It's been a blessing for Mr. Henry, though."

"What other things?"

"Well, not long after – when he was still driving hisself – he had a terrible car wreck – said he couldn't control it. With both his legs broken it's a miracle he got out before it burned. Then around Christmastime last year he went to some banquet or another and came home with a real nasty case of food poisoning."

I couldn't imagine Henry suddenly becoming so clumsy or accident prone, and said so. Petunia stopped work and stared coldly at me.

"He weren't."

My stomach started to knot. "You mean someone tried to harm him?"

She shrugged and went back to her mixing. "Dunno. Not for me to say. He's an old man."

"Petunia? Could you please make me some tea and unbuttered toast? I might be able to keep that down," said Vernita in a die-away voice. Clad in an unflattering cotton robe, she was leaning against the door jamb as if she couldn't stand erect on her own.

"Yes, Mrs. Wolfe." Petunia immediately wiped her hands and walked over to start filling an ancient kettle.

"I'm sorry you're not feeling well," I said. "Headaches can be horrible."

"I've suffered with them since I was just a slip of a girl," she murmured. "It's a cross I must bear. Petunia, I've got to go back up…"

"I'll bring you a tray as soon as it's ready, Mrs. Wolfe."

"Can I help you to your room, Vernita?" I asked, arms extended as I walked over to her in case she should crumple.

"No, I'll manage…"

"Come on. You look like you're about to topple over." Putting my arm around her shoulder in a no-nonsense grip, I turned her around and led her to the elevator.

"No," she said, digging in her heels with surprising strength. "Uncle Henry doesn't like us to use the elevator. We'll take the stairs."

I didn't think much of that, but short of picking her up bodily and shoving her into the tiny elevator I didn't have much choice. We crept up the stairs and to the door of her room; I had been right – it was the one between Henry's suite and Ryan's. She wouldn't let me come in, though; once we got there she leaned against the door and shook her head.

"No, go back down. I can get to bed well enough and my room is that messy I'd be ashamed to have you see it. Go on, Dianne... I'll probably sleep all day – it's the only thing that will cure this head of mine."

I had to – she wasn't going to budge. I nodded and walked to my own door, opening it just as Petunia came up the stairs, carrying a tray set with a delicate tea pot, cup and saucer, and a toast rack the like of which I had never seen outside of a British miniseries. She let herself into the room and closed the door silently behind her.

I went into my room and checked my cell phone just in case there had been any calls. There weren't any, which wasn't unusual; I disliked the very idea of cell phones, thinking them interrupting and intrusive, and usually left mine off altogether. Leaving it attached to the charger I turned on my computer, which lit up to the screen I had programmed to show if anyone had tried an unauthorized entry. That brought me to attention. Who had been trying to get into my computer?

Chapter Ten

ALARMED, I LOOKED around my room and was dismayed but not surprised to find that it had been searched again – just as thoroughly but not as skillfully as before. Nothing was missing, but of course there was nothing here that anyone should be interested in. I had been careful of that. Now, though, everyone knew I was Henry's granddaughter, so there really was nothing to hide.

I sat and thought for a while, trying to puzzle out why anyone would want to go through my things though my big secret was already out there, but came up empty. A bout of perusing the possibilities might work for the TV detectives, but it didn't do anything for me.

Finally I turned to my computer and, logging on to the house internet, checked my emails. A couple of contacts from friends, a magazine sounding me out for an assignment… nothing to get excited about. If I missed the assignment, that was too bad, but I wasn't leaving here without what I had come for.

The door to my room opened and closed so quickly and soundlessly I didn't have time to react before Charley was making wild shushing gestures at me.

"Please," he said in barely audible tones. "Don't scream. You don't have to be frightened – I don't want to hurt you. You're in danger and I'm here to help."

I blinked and stared at him. "Danger?"

Instantly he was by my side, one hand covering my mouth. I could feel the hard muscles of his thigh pressing against my shoulder. "Shhh. We don't know who can hear."

Nodding to show I understood – even if I didn't – I peeled his hand off my mouth and spoke in the same low whisper. "Danger? What are you talking about?"

"They're frightened of you. They're afraid the

old man will change his will and leave everything to you." He knelt by my side and tenderly cradled my head in his hands, his impossibly handsome face only inches from mine. "Please let me protect you."

Boy, he was good. His warm, liquid gaze, his gentle hands cupping my head as if it were something immeasurably precious, his sculpted lips slightly parted as if ready to kiss me... It was something straight out of one of the drugstore romance novels I had devoured in my teens. I would have suspected something amiss, though, even if I hadn't seen him *in flagrante delicto* with Vernita. Men as pretty as Charley never noticed me. Being both clear-eyed and honest, I knew I was neither beautiful nor rich enough to redirect them from their own self-centeredness.

Of course, to be honest, he had never paid me the slightest attention until everyone knew I was Henry's granddaughter. Apparently he thought I was a better bet in the money sweepstakes than Vernita.

"Protect me from what?" I asked sweetly.

"From those who might harm you. Let me take

you away from here and make sure you're safe…" One hand brushed my hair back, lingering just too long against my skin.

"And what about Vernita? Won't she miss you?"

He looked a little startled at that, but recovered and smiled. "So you've seen her, huh? She never gives me a minute's rest. I was ready to leave until you came… and I knew I had to take care of you."

"That's very kind of you," I said a little less sweetly, "but I've been looking out for myself for a long time."

"But…"

"Thank you for thinking of me, Charley." Now my voice was quiet, still mannerly, but firm. "But I have work to do."

"But Dianne…" his voice caressed my name as I might caress a mink coat – with longing but respect. "They might hurt you… Please let me take you out of here."

"You need to go, Charley." My voice was still quiet, yet a lot less mannerly. "I have to get to work."

He stood, but reluctantly. His face could have melted romantic young women and, I must admit, caused a faint flutter in even my skeptic's heart. "I'll be around, Dianne. I'll keep an eye on you, but call me if you need me."

With a soulful, yearning glance he was gone, the door closing silently behind him. Chin in my hands, I sat for a moment, unseeing eyes staring at the computer screen. Boy, that had been something else. Charley really should be in Hollywood; he simply radiated a tender machismo, and with that face he could be a star in no time. Had I been my romantic teen-aged self, I would have collapsed into a blob of Silly Putty in his hands. Being my older, more cynical self I knew how foolish that would be.

Now if it had been Ryan...

I sighed. I was really too old and too mature to be reacting to a man simply because he was ruggedly handsome and radiated masculinity like heat from a stove. Besides, if for some unknown reason he should fancy me, there was the question of Henry's fortune. Whichever of us ended up in the will, there would always be the question of love versus greed, to say nothing of who had done what to whom and why.

Sighing yet again, I pulled myself back to the present. There was at least an hour until lunch, time I should use to type up what I had learned from Petunia and Dave Mondel. Petunia's went easily, but as I transcribed my notes from Dave a funny thing happened. When I had been talking to him, he had seemed so innocent, so genuinely admiring of Henry, but when I transcribed his words without his expression or tone of voice, a totally different interpretation surfaced. I hadn't thought Dave had that much of a personality, but when it was stripped away it seemed everything changed.

What was it? Jealousy? Perhaps he thought he should have more say in the running of the company? Than who? Henry? Ryan? Without any definite example to point to it was impossible to quantify, yet still definitely uncomfortable.

I was still thinking about it as I saved the file and shut off the computer. I almost hoped he would join us for lunch so I could observe him more, but that dream was dashed. When I reached the dining room only Henry awaited me.

"Well, did you get everything down?" Henry asked, taking a long and elaborately disinterested drink of his iced tea. One thing about these Texans, there was always iced tea. I wondered that they didn't serve it with breakfast.

I sat down and squeezed a lemon into my own glass. "Yes. An interesting interview. He told me everything you told him to."

Henry actually looked affronted. "I didn't tell him anything to say."

"Well, then, what you would have wanted him to say," I replied in neutral tones. In spite of the nearly frigid air conditioning there was a heaviness in the air, a humidity I could almost squeeze out of the air with my fingers. Outside, the brilliant sunshine had vanished; now it was flat and filtered through a veil of thin, high clouds.

A place mat, silver, and a glass of tea in her hands, Petunia bustled into the room barely ahead of

Ryan.

"And what are you doing home this time of day? Is the company running itself now?"

Ryan waited until Petunia had set his place, then plopped into the chair. "Dave's there. Anything comes up, he'll call me."

Henry said nothing, but his glance was eloquent.

"So I thought I would come home for lunch."

"And?" Henry's glance became a glare.

"Okay, there's a tornado watch centered on this area until about ten tonight. Joe Don down at the station said there was some wild weather with it, so I thought I'd better come home."

"Why? You're needed down at the office! We're fine here. We've got the storm cellar in case there is a twister."

"Dave is watching things at the office and he's in touch with the mill." Ryan's voice was gentle but firm, as if he were discussing with a child. "And I know we have the storm cellar, but it wouldn't be fair of you to expect the ladies to carry you down there if needed."

"Bah, I don't need the women. Charley can help me down."

"Where is Charley?" Ryan asked in a slightly less friendly tone. "I called for him to be ready to take the car back to the garage, but Petunia said he wasn't around."

I blinked and took another sip of iced tea. Did Henry know that Charley had been to my room? That he said he had been thinking about leaving? Maybe he had left right after I rebuffed him and gone seeking more profitable hunting grounds. Had Vernita given him his walking papers too? So much for his desire to take care of me.

"Haven't seen hide nor hair of him since breakfast," Petunia said as she entered the room bearing a bowl of potato salad and a platter stacked with sandwiches. "And I've got chores for him to do."

"Perhaps he went somewhere," I said incautiously, "or maybe he left."

"Nope, no way. Everything's in the garage – every car, every truck."

Petunia handed the sandwich tray around. I took two – they looked delicious, stacked with rare-ish roast beef and all the fixings, including slices of avocado. I love avocado.

"Even his own?"

Henry snorted and took three sandwiches to go with his hefty helping of potato salad. "His own? That young puppy never owned anything in his life but his boots and jeans. If he went anywhere it'd be by foot, and he's never done that. No, he's around the place somewhere, probably looking for a way to get out of work."

My mind flashed to Vernita's closed door and her convenient headache. Was Charley in there with her, repairing fences? Or did Vernita even know about his attempt at straying? I gave a mental shrug. Either way it was no business of mine.

I looked out through the French doors; the sky seemed lower, darker. "It looks like it might rain."

"Probably will," Ryan said. "It's spring – storm season. And we can use it. Last winter was dry, and the trees show it. Don't want any fires sparking up."

"Fires are terrifying," I said with feeling, thinking of how thickly the trees grew around the house. They could be dangerous as well as protective. "They scare me, especially big ones. California's had a lot of them lately."

"Fires scare any sensible person," Henry said, chomping down on a sandwich. "But they're good for the forest."

"They burn out the litter and the dead wood," Ryan added at my look of astonishment. "Clear out the rubbish so new trees can grow strong and tall."

"It's nature's way of renewing things." A tiny bit of avocado clung to the corner of Henry's mouth. He reached up and wiped it away. "It's a good thing – when it's kept within reason."

"And since when did man's reasoning enter into anything?" Petunia asked, coming back into the room. This time she bore a platter of small iced cakes and a bowl of diced fruit. "God does what he wants to when he wants to, and man's got no say in the matter."

"Now, Petunia…" Ryan began, but she stomped

toward the door.

"Don't you 'now Petunia' me, Ryan Cable. I've got my work and Charley's to do and no time to hang around flappin' my jaw. Just leave everything on the table and I'll get it later."

I almost offered to help – not because I like kitchen work, but because I wanted to hear more of Petunia's stories about my mother and grandmother. She didn't seem in a mood to chat, though, so instead I finished cleaning my plate and reached for the dessert platter. I really was going to gain weight here if I didn't watch myself. After two little iced cakes and a handful of wonderful dark purplish-blue grapes, I decided I didn't care. Time enough to worry about my waistline when I was back home.

"Well, missy," Henry said at last. "You want to get back to work?"

What I really wanted was a nap, but I nodded my head. "I'll just go get my tablet and notepad."

"No need. There's paper in my office. We can work there."

Without waiting for an answer, Henry turned

and wheeled himself out the door. Leaning back in his chair, Ryan chuckled.

"That's Henry."

"Dictatorial sort, isn't he?"

"He's earned it. Started with next to nothing. Poor kid, little schooling, but still built an empire."

I glared at him. "And managed to alienate his only remaining family."

His face hardened a little. "Your mother was the one who left."

"He didn't ask her back. He wouldn't even accept her letters."

"I believe him when he says there were no letters. And he did keep an eye on her. If she'd really needed anything he'd have arranged it."

A cauldron of emotions – most bitter and angry – churned within me. Memories of our straightened circumstances, of things we had wanted that we had to do without, of vacations not taken, little luxuries denied... Then after their sudden, shattering deaths, my loneliness, heartbreak, isolation – the terrible feeling of not having a single soul in the world...

I bit my lips before speaking. "Then he had to know that my father was an honorable man, and that he and my mother were very much in love. But he just watched…"

Realization washed over me in a dirty, disgusting wave.

"Through you. You were the one who checked up on us."

There was no way he could have missed the poison, the hatred in my voice. He stood up slowly and took a step toward me, then reconsidered taking another one. "In later years, yes. On occasion. And I tried to make him see reason, to contact your mother, but he wouldn't. Said she was the one who left. Said he would welcome her when she asked to come home."

"But he refused..."

Suddenly unwilling to cope with any of this any longer, I whirled about, ready to run, but was stopped as he grabbed both my forearms in a gentle grip.

"Dianne…"

"Let me go, you – you Peeping Tom!"

He didn't, but instead pulled me closer until our faces were only inches apart. "Just listen to me a minute. Yes, I went right after your parents' accident. I kept going back to check on you, even after Henry told me to let the detective keep watch. You impressed me, Dianne. I tried to think of a way to meet you, to get to know you, but I knew as soon as you found out my connection to Henry you'd send me packing. I was the one who suggested your coming here to Henry…"

"Why? Why on earth would you do that?" I snapped, conveniently ignoring that I had schemed to get here on my own.

"Because I – I'm attracted to you." His voice was low and caressing, the kind of voice a woman dreams of hearing. "I have been since the first day I saw you. I…" He leaned even more forward, coming close enough to kiss me.

I could have leaned in to make the kiss easier, but then sanity intervened. With a sudden jerk I pulled free and ran from the room, wishing I had never come to Wolfe House.

No, that wasn't quite true, I had to admit even as I skittered up the stairs. Of course I had to leave now, but I wasn't sorry I had come. I could fight Henry for the ring and the portrait from California, perhaps even better than I could here with the distraction of Ryan Cable staring me in the face. I mean, how stupid could I be? I'd known him just a day or two, a length of time that could be just as easily counted in hours, and I was as moony over him as a teenager over a movie star. Bert and I had known each other for years, and had taken almost a year to decide to marry; that had been safe and sane and sensible, for all that our marriage had been so tragically short. By comparison, I feared that I would go running to Ryan Cable the minute he crooked his finger at me.

Worst of all, I couldn't say why. It was an attraction that came from someplace so deep in my soul I couldn't analyze it.

At the top of the stairs I finally remembered that Henry was downstairs waiting for me. Well, he could just wait. I was going to get out of here. This place was messing with my mind. No – I had to be honest. It was Ryan who was messing with my mind. I would pack and go tonight, tomorrow at the latest, and if Henry wanted to sue me for breach of contract, let him.

Chapter Eleven

BUT THERE WAS something I wanted to do first. Instead of going to my room, I went to my mother's. The door was still unlocked, the drapes still drawn. I turned on the light, then closed the door behind me. Since my secret had never really been one, surely there could be no objection to my going inside; there was no need to be secretive any longer.

The whole room was almost heart-stoppingly beautiful, yet soulless. All evidence that this room had once housed a vibrant girl had been siphoned away, leaving nothing but a pretty shell, like a department store display, or perhaps a movie set. Something static and artificial. It was hard to believe that anyone as vibrant and alive as my mother had ever lived here. It seemed she should have left some imprint of her energy, her personality on this elegant, sad room.

There was nothing. Even the portrait, while a masterpiece of the portraitist's art, was the same, lifeless and soulless, yet so lifelike that I found myself willing it to speak. There was so much I wanted to know, questions I had not known to ask when it would have been possible - not that she would necessarily have been willing to answer.

One by one I opened the drawers, but aside from some floral paper lining they were empty. So was the closet. Two large suitcases, a matched pair, huddled lonely in a corner; they too were empty. On one side of the vanity top were a fancy silver brush and comb and a matching bottle obviously meant for perfume. On the other was the ornate jewelry box that had reputedly once belonged to an Italian princess. Mother had described it to me often when I was a child – I had been fascinated by the idea of a box being an intricate puzzle of drawers, false bottoms, and hidey holes. I knew where all of them were, but it didn't make any difference. The box was completely empty.

So not only was the ring missing, but so were her mother's diamond earrings that had become hers on her sixteenth birthday, and the strand of pearls that had been her grandmother's... Even her Girl Scout pin was gone. It was as if the entire box had been vacuumed, for not even a shred of dust collected in its corners. I could have wept to find that the hidden switch to the false bottom of the chest was broken; it hurt to know that this beautiful thing that had lasted over several centuries was wounded. It hurt almost as much as finding my mother's jewelry gone.

An empty vase of exquisite porcelain rested on top of the lace scarf that covered the chest of drawers. A crystal water jug and glass sat on the pristine nightstand beside a delicate if somewhat impractical lamp. The bed itself was covered with a pale lilac spread, but there were no sheets beneath it.

There was nothing of my mother here.

If only the walls and furniture could talk... If the portrait... I looked at it, willing it to speak, to impart something, to acknowledge me in some way, but it merely hung silent and serene, looking over my head into nothingness.

There was nothing here to keep me, not in this room, not in Wolfe House. Turning off the light, I peeked out, making sure the landing was empty before I slipped out to my own room. I hadn't closed the curtains before going down to lunch and was astonished at the change in the weather just in the time I had been in my mother's room. The low, dark sky had intensified, until it seemed that the clouds would catch on the roof, and it was dark enough to be almost night instead of mid-afternoon.

I had intended to start packing, but I was startled to see that my luggage was gone from the corner, and that my laptop was no longer on the desk, nor my nightgown on the bed. The reality was astonishing. Where had everything gone? I gasped, and that tiny sliver of time sealed my fate.

I had been stupid. It never occurred to me that if I could walk soundlessly over the wooden floors so could someone else. The blow that glanced off my skull sent me down in a whirlpool of swirling blackness.

* * * * *

Motion. Slow, jerky, painful motion. My left arm ached as it was stretched to its limit. There was a cruel band around my wrist as someone or something seemed to be trying to jerk my arm out of its socket. The darkness still swallowed me, but there were sensations - the polished wood floor sliding beneath me, a dull, persistent throbbing in my head, the sharp pain in my arm... I forced my eyes open, but there was only blackness. Had I been stricken blind? Or blindfolded?

I cried out in fear, and the tugging on my arm ceased. I cried out again, and tried to pull my arm back. For a moment the grip tightened, then abruptly loosed, allowing my arm to fall to the floor. The movement made me dizzy and I closed my eyes again, keeping them that way until the nausea roiling in my stomach subsided. Throbbing, my head felt as if it might fall off and my ears rang.

Once I was in control again I realized I was neither blind nor blindfolded; my face had been down on the floor but now there was light. I forced my eyes open and this time I could see. I was on the landing, right beside the open elevator and uncomfortably close to the stairs. One more jerk on my arm, I thought passionlessly, and I would have been inside. Or over the edge.

There was something more intruding into my field of vision, something that was much more unsettling. A pair of shoes. Men's shoes. I raised my head; the movement sent stabbing pains through my brain and made my stomach swim, but they were secondary to what I saw.

Henry Wolfe.

My grandfather.

Standing over me, looking down as if a god from Olympus.

"You can walk," I said rather stupidly.

He bent over me and I flinched. It would take so little to send me hurtling down that long flight of steps. Could I stop or even survive such a horrific tumble? I didn't know.

"Not well," he said in a low voice, taking one of

my wrists in his large, knotted hands. "Not well enough to lift you. Can you stand?"

"Yes," I answered, as much to convince myself as him. After the first nauseating rush of vertigo, though, standing was not as difficult as I had feared. Between Henry's steadying hands and a firm grip on the bannister it wasn't difficult to scramble into a standing position.

"Come. Quickly," he whispered, wrapping one strong arm around my waist and hurrying me through the open door into his room.

It was, I realized, the light from his room that I had seen. The sconces on the landing were all off.

He closed the door behind us and, planting me firmly on the edge of the bed, seated himself in his wheelchair with a slight grunt.

"How long have you been able to walk?" I asked in accusing tones. "Why do you let everyone think you're crippled?"

"Because I don't trust anyone," he grumbled in return. "And don't you go telling anyone, either."

Perhaps something had been jarred loose in my

brain, for suddenly things were rearranging themselves in different patterns. "Were you the one who hit me?"

"Hit you?"

"I'm not in the habit of lying down on the landing floor." My voice was tart. "Did you see anyone?"

"No. I heard what sounded like a scuffle, but by the time I got to the door there was just you. I thought you had fainted."

"I didn't faint. I went to look at my mother's room… it's so sad. What became of all her things?"

He looked blankly at me. "What do you mean? Everything's in there. It's just as it always was."

"No. The furniture's there, but her clothes and jewelry are all gone. Everything's empty."

His face darkened angrily. "That's not possible! I said everything was to be left right where it was." He was so obviously upset that I believed him.

"When was the last time you were in there?"

"I take a peek every now and then, just to make sure it's cleaned properly, but haven't set foot in there since the night she ran away."

From the doorway it wouldn't be possible to see that things had changed. "Who could have taken her things?"

Suddenly Henry slumped in on himself, becoming very old in the process. "Any number of people. We've had workmen in the place, thrown parties and had caterers, even a few business meetings. Until my accident Wolfe House was known for its hospitality."

Mother had mentioned the many parties at her home. The secret catch on the Italian princess' jewel box had been broken. That could have been done by someone prowling around. If no one had checked on Mother's room her stuff could have been gone for years. Or... an ugly thought raised its head. Could Billy Don have taken her things in some sort of perverted revenge or some other unwholesome reason I didn't really want to think about? It would have been difficult for him, but not impossible.

"Did Billy Don Prendergast come to those parties?"

It was as if Henry read my mind, for he shot me a blistering look. "He's always been welcome in this house, but he wouldn't do anything like that. No way."

I reserved judgement on that, but there were other things that needed immediate attention more. Billy Don I could deal with later.

"After I left Mother's room I went into mine..." I stopped for a moment, seeing again that bare and denuded space. "And all my stuff was gone too."

"Gone?"

"Yes. Bags, laptop, everything. I mean, I didn't look in the drawers, but I'll bet they're empty. Like I had never been here. Or... like I had left. Who wants to get rid of me, Henry?"

"I don't know," he said softly, studying his hands. "Perhaps the same one who tried to kill me."

"Kill...? Your accidents?"

"Yep. I may be old, but I'm not stupid. Figured if they thought I was a weak old man in a wheelchair they'd get careless. Didn't think it would go on so long." Failure was thick in his voice, as was a definite self-loathing. Henry Wolfe didn't like not being in control of everything.

"Is that why you brought me here?"

"Sort of. I thought if you were here I could keep you safe."

"Keep me…?" This was an aspect of Henry that I had never even imagined. My inner world seemed to be crumbling and refashioning itself. My stomach knotted. "So you thought I might be in danger?"

"Yep. Fine mess I've made of that."

"But why…? You acted like you hated me."

He smiled, and there was a ghost of the charismatic young man he must have been when my grandmother fell in love with him. "I knew how you felt about me. How would you have felt if I suddenly held out my arms and said come home?"

I couldn't restrain a wry smile. "I'd have thought you had something up your sleeve and probably run the other way. What made you think I was in danger?"

"You know I had you and your mother watched." Henry drew in a deep breath, then let it

158

out. "I don't think your parents' deaths were an accident."

The world swirled around me in a kaleidoscope of colors and sounds and feelings. I had had the same conviction, only to have it dismissed by the police. They had been kind, but obviously thought me an irrational, grief-stricken daughter. Well, maybe I had been, but I could not shake the feeling. My dad had been a very good driver. It wasn't possible he could have caused such a catastrophic one car wreck.

"I'd been waiting for Stephanie to say she wanted to come home..." His voice was tragic. "Like a stupid fool I waited too long. I wasn't going to make the same mistake with you. And look now. I've put you in danger."

"We're going to get out of this. We're going to leave here. Once we're far away and both safe then we can figure out who's behind this," I said, my spine stiffening. There were still things Henry and I had to work out, but first we had to stay alive.

"I'm not going to run away!" His expression

was fierce enough to scare a Cossack. I didn't care. I'd just found my grandfather, and I wasn't going to lose him, not like this.

"Well, I am, and I'm taking you with me. You can do what you want once this is settled and we're safe. All the cars are in the barn? Where are the keys?"

"There's a box on the wall next to the people door."

"Come on. Let's go."

He shook his head. "You go. I'm too slow. I'll just hold you back, and I don't think I can make it as far as the barn."

I hated to leave him, but time seemed to be pushing with an almost physical force. The air itself seemed thick with fear and the wind sounded almost as if it were crying 'hurry, hurry.'

"Okay. Can you get down to the front door? I'll get something and pick you up there."

He hesitated for a moment, then nodded. "I'll get there. Wait a minute!" He reached under his pillow and brought out a .45 Ruger automatic. It was an

160

older 1911 model but obviously impeccably maintained. "Do you know how to use this?"

"Of course. Daddy taught me how to shoot when I was still in elementary school." Taking the gun, I slipped it into the back of my waistband where the metal lay cold and comforting against my flesh. With my loose shirt over it the gun shouldn't be visible.

"Careful! There's a round in the chamber."

"Is the safety on?"

"Of course," he answered indignantly.

"Then there's nothing to worry about." I stood and, surprising both of us, dropped a light kiss on his forehead. "We'll beat this. I'll meet you downstairs in a few minutes."

As a writer-for-hire, I've been in some less-than-comfortable situations, but never one as flat terrifying as going down the dark well of the stairs and out the front door of the seemingly deserted house.

The weather was more frightening. Now the clouds seemed to be within reach, and they and even the air itself were a dark and incredible green. This was not good. Raindrops so big they felt like small rocks were falling, and they hurt pounding against my skin. The barn was some fifty yards away, so I set out with a run that would have garnered cheers on a football field.

A car was speeding down the road, heading directly for me.

Charley? Was he coming back for me? I kind of wished I hadn't been so dismissive of him, especially since now he could help me get Henry out of here. I knew that seemed contradictory considering how I felt about him – and I still distrusted him – but Daddy had always said that in an emergency you have to use what you've got.

The question was moot, because it wasn't Charley. The car sped up, then braked to a halt so close in front of me I had to stop abruptly to keep from running into the side of the hood. No time to move, no time to change direction, no time for anything because he was getting out of the car, but I knew who it was before he stepped out.

Ryan. The man who had watched me and my life for I don't know how long.

Ryan. The man my grandfather had trusted with his business and with his life.

Ryan. The man who attracted me more than any other man ever had.

Ryan. The heir.

Ryan. The only man who would benefit if both Henry and I died.

Chapter Twelve

"STOP RIGHT THERE," I shouted, stepping back. I didn't want him to know I had the gun. While I was a decent shot and would defend Henry's and my life with any means possible, the idea of actually shooting a person – shooting Ryan – was abhorrent.

"What the devil are you doing out here?" Ryan said, coming around the front of the car. At first the rain spotted his shirt, then soaked it, plastering it to his body. The fine cloth molded over his muscles and he appeared to be nearly naked from the waist up.

I took a deep breath and focused my thoughts. "You stay right where you are! Henry and I are getting out of here."

Confusion clouded his face even as he kept walking. I could feel the gun beneath the soaked cloth of my shirt, but was powerless to draw it. Some big hot-shot defender I was.

"Out of here? My God, Dianne, look at the sky! There's a tornado coming."

Tornado? Why had I thought Texas was always hot and dry? All we had had since I arrived was rain and storms and now a tornado?

He took another step forward, grabbed my shoulders, and gave me a shake. Then, in a move that shook me to the depths of my being, he bent and kissed me, his lips almost devouring mine. His hands were sizzlingly hot even through my wet shirt and I was so unnerved by his kiss I could have melted like sugar in the rain that pelted us unmercifully, slithering down our bodies like cold tongues.

"You can go anywhere you want," he shouted over the howl of the wind. "As soon as this weather has broken! Get back in the house."

"No, we're going to leave now..." I screamed, but any explanation I could give was torn away by the wind.

Ryan swore, his face going pale. His fingers

clamped painfully on my arms as he whirled me around. I felt like screaming, but the wind that whipped my hair around also seemed to suck the breath from my body.

The clouds had sunk even lower while the green darkened until it was almost black. The worst thing was that no more than a couple of miles away a circle had begun to form, lazily pulling the low sullen clouds into a disk-like shape. It rotated slowly, like a flying saucer in a bad movie, becoming bigger and thicker with every turn.

The wind went from merely a loud noise to the throbbing urgency of a train surging toward us.

We watched in horror as the center of the disk began to drop and stretch, a single finger stretching to touch the earth, flinging branches about as it reached the treetops.

I had seen such things on TV and the movies, of course, but never in real life. It was fascinating, hypnotic, terrifying... In those few seconds - no more than two or three - the entire world had changed.

Ryan swore again, and then gave me a not-so-gentle shove. "The storm cellar! Now!"

I had seen the storm cellar of course, but only as a sod covered lump with a semi-horizontal door not far from the barn. "Henry," I screamed over the roar of the wind. "Henry's in the house. So're your mother and Petunia..."

"I'll get them! You get into the storm cellar," he screamed, then took off at a flat run toward the house.

I didn't need to be told twice. I set off across the grass, feeling as if I were running against a wall intent on pushing me backward, I couldn't catch my breath, the ground was wet and slick beneath my feet, I was slipping, sliding...

"Dianne! Help!" The words were weak, barely audible over the pulsing roar of the storm.

Almost halfway between the barn and the storm cellar I slithered to a stop, leaning into the wind as if against a solid object. Holding heavily onto the open barn door, Vernita looked as if she could barely stand. Piteously she waved at me. "Help me, Dianne..."

I didn't like the woman. I was scared to death. There was a tornado, a full-fledged one now stripping the tops of trees on its way to the ground, and it was bearing down on us.

There was only one thing I could do. I changed direction and covered the yards between me and the barn, then stepped inside. There was wind in here, too, clawing through the open doors and even the chinks between the boards, but after the maelstrom outside it felt wonderful.

Vernita was nowhere in sight. All I could see was a pickup and an older sedan, parked neatly against the wall.

"Vernita? Where are you?"

"Here. Hurry." Her voice sounded thin and die-away, barely audible over the roar of the storm.

I looked around, but there was nothing in the barn that one wouldn't expect. Where was Vernita? Why hadn't she waited for me by the door? Was she ill? Injured? Could I get her to the storm cellar in time? My stomach began to knot in fear again. If I couldn't find her and get us to the cellar, we were in very real danger of dying an extremely nasty death.

In the middle of the barn a door hung open and a faint glow of light came from within. Vernita was in there, but the instant I stepped in it became obvious she was not alone. Now I knew where Charley was, and was equally as sure that he could never go anywhere else again, at least not under his own power.

He lay crumpled in the corner, contorted into a knot that no living person could maintain. His face was pressed against the dirty concrete floor, but it wasn't beautiful anymore. Contorted in the throes of death, his mouth gaped open and dust lay unbothering on his staring eyes.

My stomach clenched with equal parts dismay and fear.

I had good reason to be afraid. Vernita, now vigorous, stood just inside the door.

"Come in, Dianne," she said in the most cordial of tones that were in direct variance with the gun she jabbed into my ribs. "Go over next to Charley, will you?"

I'm neither cowardly nor weak, but I'm not stupid, either. When someone jabs a gun against you, you move. I did move close to Charley – the thing that had been Charley – but was careful to stand far enough away that his out-flung hand did not touch my shoe. The hand that had recently touched my cheek in a fair counterfeit of affection. I couldn't bear that.

"You killed him. You killed Charley."

"Of course I did. Stupid boy. He really thought I would make him rich when Ryan inherits. Then he found out you were Uncle Henry's long lost granddaughter and figured his chances would be better with you... Fool." Her voice dripped with sarcasm.

"My bags..." I stared stupidly. Next to Charley's body stood my two suitcases, tote bag, and purse. "How did they get here?"

"Charlie brought them down so you two could run away together." Vernita gave a trilling little laugh. "At least, that's what people will think. I looked for your wallet. It wasn't in your purse, so you must have it on you."

I did, in my pocket – an old habit – but I wasn't going to tell her that. "I never…"

Vernita smiled. It was horrible in its ordinariness. "But of course you did. Don't you know he fell in love with you and you two planned to leave? I don't know what you quarreled about, but you shot him and then realizing what you had done, you shot yourself." She waggled the gun as if I couldn't get what she was planning. "It's tragic, of course, but so very neat. If the storm leaves anything of either of you, that is."

Neat indeed. With me dead, there would be no one who knew the truth. It would have been comforting in a weird kind of way to believe that she was totally mad, but she wasn't. She was coldly, rationally, indubitably sane… and a murderer. Didn't someone say that the second murder was always easier?

"Why?"

"Come now, Dianne, you can't be that stupid. Henry has been mooning about you ever since you got here. I can't have him changing his will. I had to work much too hard to ensure that Ryan would be his heir. When Henry dies I'll be the real mistress of Wolfe House." Her eyes glowed with the promise of such a future.

"But why kill Charley? You loved him…"

"Hardly. He was convenient." She was dismissive. "He was quick enough to dump me when I told him you had changed your mind and wanted to meet him in the barn so you could go away together. Poor fool begged me to take him back once I got him down here, as if I would have kept him around in the first place. When Ryan inherits I'll be socializing with rich people, important people, people who really count. I'll be the hostess instead of just the housekeeper. Then they'll know how special I really am."

"But how did my bags get down here? Did Charley really bring them? Petunia must have seen…"

I was armed, I told myself. I didn't have to be afraid. If only I could get to the gun in the small of my back before she shot me. She was completely capable of shooting me, but could I shoot her? I honestly didn't know. I did know I could hopefully scare her... like she was scaring me.

"I sent Petunia into Longview on an errand right after lunch. She might not even come back today." Slowly she raised the pistol and sighted down the barrel at my head. "And I packed up your room. Made sure nothing was left. Then I brought out the bags. Don't think someone will come rescue you, because I was very careful that nobody saw. Ryan was at the mill, Henry was in his office. I'm very organized, you see."

"Did you kill my parents?" I asked somewhat desperately.

She shrugged and raised her voice against the increasing wind. "My late husband – the first one – was a beast, but he had some friends who have been helpful from time to time. What made you not go with them that night? It made things very inconvenient."

So Henry and I had been right. My parents'

deaths hadn't been an accident. Not that it made much difference at the moment.

"Henry and Ryan are in the house. They'll be killed when the tornado hits. We've got to help them."

That shook her! Her eyes widened and the tip of the gun trembled. "You're lying. Petunia's gone and I don't care about Henry. That just means Ryan will inherit the sooner. It's not nice to lie, you know. He's at the mill, and they have a big storm cellar there."

"He is here," I cried desperately. "I just spoke to him. He's gone in the house to get Henry. We've got to get to the storm cellar!"

"Liar! He told me…" She took a deep breath and visibly pulled herself together as she gave a deprecating little laugh. "Well played, but I don't believe you. But, just in case it makes you feel a little better before you die, Ryan is infatuated with you. Silly boy. He'll get over it, though." She smiled, then tightened her finger around the trigger.

"No!" It must have been I who shouted, but it

didn't sound like me. I wasn't paying much attention to anything except that huge empty hole at the end of the gun.

For a moment the wail of the wind vanished in the thunder of a shot.

Chapter Thirteen

CLOSING MY EYES, I had flung myself down, hoping against hope to out-speed the bullet. Not logical, nor even physically possible, but when your death is imminent, you will try anything to gain just a few more moments of life. I hit the concrete floor with a painful thud that drove the breath from my body and a cloud of dust up my nose, but could not feel any wound. Of course, some say that you never feel it when you get shot. The pain theoretically comes later, after you've survived. If you survive.

Wondering if I could see, I cautiously opened one eye and was surprised by the sight of Ryan wrestling with his mother and pushing her arm upward. He must have been able to deflect her aim just enough to miss me. Another shot went through the ceiling before he could wrest the gun from her grip. I found it vaguely fascinating that there was an eruption of brilliant flame from the barrel, just like in the movies. Entwined in a combative embrace, mother and son fell across Charley's body with a squishy thud that I would hear in my nightmares.

His face grey with fatigue, Henry shuffled across the floor towards me until he was stopped by Ryan, who shoved the pistol into Henry's hand. "Watch her," he shouted over the roaring wind, then knelt and gathered me into his arms.

It was a most pleasurable sensation, almost as if I were weightless.

"What the devil do you think you're doing, Ryan?" Vernita spat. "Get that gun back now."

He ignored her.

"Dianne! Can you hear me? Are you hurt?" Ryan's voice was almost frantic as he caressed my face.

Mentally I ran down my body. Hands moved, feet moved, eyes blinked... no pain, no feeling of wetness nor faintness from loss of blood... Just a throbbing headache, but I'd had that since being knocked in the head.

"I don't think so." I blinked and came fully back to the present. I was alive and, save for what would probably be a spectacular couple of bruises, unhurt. Above me Ryan's face was taut with fear, but when I smiled at him it relaxed and he smiled back. He did have the most beautiful smile.

"Ryan, you listen to me!" Vernita's voice had risen to a shrill edge that almost rivaled the wind.

"Is she all right?" Henry shouted over the nearly deafening wind. He was trembling a little, but his aim at Vernita was rock solid.

"I'm fine, Grandfather."

I hadn't intended to say it. I had never intended to say it, but once it was done it felt right.

Above even the noise of the wind there were the screams of tortured wood giving way. Around us the barn shuddered as if it were a living thing undergoing physical assault.

"She's starting to go!" Henry said. "Come on, we've got to get to a safe place."

Ryan helped me to my feet, then looked at

Henry, his face grim. "It's almost on top of us! We'll never make the storm cellar in time."

Henry – Grandfather – glanced over at us; unbelievably, a twinkle of amusement shone in his eyes. "Ryan, that corner – " he gestured to the farthest regions of the room " – under all that junk there's a trap door. Open it."

Luckily there wasn't much in the corner – a couple of boxes, some ancient wooden chairs, and unidentifiable trash. Ryan and I tossed it all out of the way almost instantly. In the concrete floor was a large, metal bound square with a heavy ring set into it. Ryan yanked at the ring and the trap door lifted with hardly a screech.

"Now," Henry said, waving the gun at a disconcertingly composed Vernita. His voice trembled a little from age and fatigue, but it still radiated authority. "Down, Vernita. Ryan, go after her. Keep her out of mischief."

Ryan followed his mother down what looked like a dangerously rickety stair.

"Now you, girl," he ordered me.

"You're going to need help…" I said as the roof of the inner room began to quiver and loosen.

"Get down there! I'll get myself down."

And he did, grunting as he pulled the heavy door down just as the screaming wind began to remove the boards one by one, sending them flying through the air like spears. The darkness was absolute. Wherever we were – a cellar? a storeroom? – smelled damp and musty and far too much like a grave for my tastes. I hoped it wasn't an omen.

Once I had reached the bottom of the stairs I stepped aside so Henry – Grandfather – could come down. He had made the stairs slowly, but once he hit the bottom he kept moving, going behind me along the wall.

"Everyone stay right where you are," he ordered.

"Ryan, grab that gun!"

"Why, Mom? What did you think you were doing?" In the dark Ryan's voice sounded almost plaintive.

There was a sound of fumbling, then a clink of glass and the scrape of a match and suddenly the room was filled with a watery, golden light. I had never seen anything more beautiful.

That's not true. I did, and at that exact same moment. It was the look in Ryan's eyes as his gaze found mine, a look I had never seen before. Though he had indeed loved me, Bert had never looked at me with that overpowering expression of love, not even on our wedding day. My world shifted and resettled itself into an unexpected but so welcome pattern.

"There, that's better," Henry said, picking up the gun again and putting it in his pocket. "Handy thing, a coal oil lamp."

Ryan moved to my side and took my hand in his. "What is this place, Uncle Henry? I didn't even know it was down here."

"There's no reason you have to know everything," he replied with the ghost of a smile. "This old place has a lot of secrets."

"But the lamp… What have you been up to?"

Henry laughed. "The lamp's down here as a precaution. Kept one ready to light for years. Never really needed it until now."

"What was this originally?" I asked, happy to feel Ryan's arm move from alongside mine to drape protectively about my shoulders. I would have hated to be down here alone. The chamber was about twelve feet square and maybe eight feet high, made fully of concrete. There was a rough bench against one wall and nothing else except for the equally rough table on which the lamp stood. At least, that was all I could see. The lamp did its best, but still there were shadows lurking beyond its yellowish glow.

"Dunno for sure," Henry said, walking to the bench and sitting down with a sigh. He looked exhausted. "Used to be tales that bootleggers hid their booze here during Prohibition. Also heard it was a slave hole, but don't think that's true. This place isn't old enough. Not many slaves in this area, anyway. Could have been used for almost anything, I guess. Depends on what you want to hide away."

"Are you all right, Henry? Grandfather?" I added tentatively, and was rewarded by a brief hug from Ryan.

"This is not about a history lesson," Vernita snapped, "and this family reunion is getting downright sickening. I told you what to do, Ryan, so hop to it, boy!"

Ryan turned to look at his mother, his expression unreadable.

"I'm okay, Dianne," Henry answered, then looked across to Vernita, the fatigue on his face vanishing only to be replaced by the hard, penetrating look of a businessman. "Just what in the Sam Hill did you think you were doing, Vernita? You killed Charley. Wasn't he giving you enough?"

If anything, Vernita was cool. She stood on the opposite side of the room, as relaxed and composed as if she were in the parlor in the house. "Now what makes you think a horrid thing like that, Uncle Henry? Charley was devoted to me, and our dear Dianne just couldn't stand that, so when he wouldn't leave with her, she killed him."

I opened my mouth to protest, but was stopped by the ungentle pressure of Ryan's fingers digging into my shoulder.

"I don't believe you, Vernita," Henry said calmly.

The air filled with a tense silence almost as thick as the dust. The room was solid, for outside the storm was nothing more than a faint roar. I leaned in closer to Ryan, finding comfort in the muscular solidity of his body against mine.

"She said she had my parents killed."

Sudden anger as dangerous as fire flew from Henry's eyes. "I wondered, but I didn't think even you could sink that low, Vernita."

The housekeeper shrugged. "The woman is obviously off her rocker, Uncle Henry. Why would I do that?"

"To make sure that your son inherited."

"I was supposed to be with them that night," I said. The thickness in my voice was just because of the dust. At least, that's what I wanted to think. How much air was there in this concrete tomb? And when would it run out? I stole a glance at the lamp, but the flame still burned steadily.

Without warning the slight noise of the storm

ceased.

"It's over," I said, looking up at the stained concrete ceiling. Now maybe we could get out of here. I didn't know if it was a sudden attack of claustrophobia or a distaste for being in an enclosed space with a murderess who had just tried to kill me, but I wanted out.

"Better stay for a minute," Henry said. "Maybe it's just the center of the storm, or maybe that thing will turn around and come back. You can't outguess a tornado."

"I'm going to check if the door will open," Ryan said, going up the first few stairs. "If there's a pile of stuff on top of it we're in trouble."

"You mean we might be trapped?" My voice was unpleasantly squeaky.

"Stay put, Ryan. Don't have to worry about that. There's a tunnel back up under the stairs that comes out pretty far back in the woods. It was in fair to middlin' shape the last time I checked."

"Is there anything else I don't know?" Ryan asked, his voice holding a bit of an edge.

"Probably." Incredibly, Henry chuckled, the last thing I would have expected anyone to do in this situation. "An old dog never shows all his tricks."

Ryan came back to stand by me and replaced his arm around my shoulders, for which I was glad. I didn't know if I could stand so many revelations in such a short time.

But there was something I had to know.

"You took my mother's ring, didn't you?"

Vernita laughed as if that were the stupidest question in the world. "Of course I did, you stupid girl. She had her white trash boyfriend, so why did she need a ring like that?"

I would have scratched her eyes out then and there if Ryan hadn't been holding me so tightly I couldn't even wiggle. But there was worse to come.

"I even let Uncle Henry – " her voice all but dripped with sarcasm " – think that she had taken all her jewelry with her."

"Mom," Ryan's voice was so tight it almost hid the pain lurking there. "Why? Why did you do all that?"

"For us, of course. Why should they have all the money and status and pretty things we should have? If Henry had played fair with me none of this would have been necessary."

"Uncle Henry has been more than fair..."

"You never had any ambition," she said dismissively. "You're a weakling, just like Robert was."

"You returned my mother's letters," I said softly, incapable of comprehending the depths of this woman's villainy.

"And why shouldn't I?" She laughed scornfully. "It was the practical thing to do. He was so sentimental about her he would have brought her back, and then where would Ryan and I have been?"

Henry cleared his throat. "You destroyed my letters to Stephanie, didn't you?"

"You wrote Mother?" I asked, astonished.

"Yes. A couple of times. In the beginning, after you were born. I didn't know she never got them. How could you do such a thing, Vernita?"

She shrugged with a dismissive arrogance.

"Easily. I worked hard to look after you and make sure Ryan would be your heir. I didn't need that snotty little miss coming back and messing everything up. I worried that you'd write her from the office and I wouldn't be able to catch it from there, but you're such an old stick-in-the-mud, Henry. You do personal things at home and business things at the office. So predictable. Oh, you were so easy to deceive," she crooned. "And I enjoyed every minute of it. Dear Uncle Henry, keeping us tied to you, making us dance to your tune…"

"I took you and Ryan in and gave you a home." Henry's voice sank deeper and deeper as the look on his face became more murderous. "I paid for Ryan's education. I gave him a job, and a darned good one at that."

"Yes, and you never let us forget any of it. We were always the poor relations, here on your charity." She all but spat the word.

"I didn't think you could be so vicious, Vernita," Henry said slowly. "Even though you tried to kill me."

Ryan was conspicuously silent.

"You're an old man, Henry Wolfe. A mean old man, and you were taking such a long time about dying. Well, that's all over. Thanks to the storm everything's changed and we can do what we want. Go on, Ryan, get the gun and take care of them. Precious Miss Dianne killed Charley – she might as well kill Henry too."

For a heartbeat everything within me stopped. Ryan? Was he part of this horror? He was the one who had 'kept an eye' on me in California. Had he kept an eye on my parents too? A deadly eye? And what about Henry? He seemed genuinely fond of the old man, but now I didn't believe much of anything.

"Won't wash, Vernita," Henry said with a slow sadness.

"Oh, shut up you blathering old fool," Vernita snapped. "No one cares what you think any more. Ryan, turn loose of that stupid girl and get his gun. Now!"

The moment seemed to stretch on forever. The silence was so profound I could hear the lamp wick crackling as it burned.

Then I remembered. It was amazing that I had forgotten I was armed. Ryan might take away Henry's gun – he was an old man and not overly strong – but Henry's .45 was still in the small of my back. I took a step sideways, but Ryan's grip just became that much harder. So I leaned back into Ryan's embrace, but put my hand on my hip, ready to slip under my shirt and grab the gun if necessary.

Whenever the time came to do something, I would do it. Whatever it might be.

"No, Mom."

Vernita glared at him with a look that could have set fires. "What did you say, young man? I'm your mother. I raised you. Everything I've done I've done for you. Now do what I tell you."

"No, Mom. Everything you did you did for yourself. Uncle Henry tried to tell me, but I didn't believe him. I wanted to prove him wrong."

"He really did try to prove you innocent, you know," Henry said. "He believed in you. Frankly, I didn't want to believe you could be so evil."

"You're a murderess." The words came slowly from Ryan's mouth, painfully, as if they cut his flesh on the way out. "I've suspected it for a while."

"You lose, Vernita." Henry stood up, one joint at a time. "Ryan came to me some time ago. He was worried about you. Not because you were sleeping with young Charley – that was just trashy – but because you were starting to talk crazy. Then Stephanie and her husband were killed in that accident, when Dianne here was supposed to be with them. It was only pure old good luck that she wasn't. Then I had my 'accidents,' and that made it seem much more like the truth. Ryan and I concocted a plan to see if what we thought might be true." Henry's voice ached with sadness.

"So what? No one will ever know about it… Ryan's your heir. That means he'll inherit and I'll be the lady of Wolfe House."

"Mom…" Ryan's voice was hollow. "I don't understand why you did this. Uncle Henry did well by us."

"And he could have taken everything away with

a snap of his fingers, leaving us with nothing again! Your father was a no good. Oh, we lived high with him, but when he was killed we were left without anything."

"Uncle Robert…"

"Robert Coffey was a weakling, content to live on nothing!" Vernita snapped. Her color was rising right along with her anger. Even in the golden light of the oil lamp her face glowed a furious red and, if this had been a cartoon, steam would have been rising from her ears. Tiny bubbles of spittle foamed in the corners of her mouth. "He left us barely enough to survive on. I'm tired of having nothing, and I'm tired of being nobody, and I'm tired of always being the loser, so you take care of them both right now!"

"You can have both of us killed, Vernita, even if Ryan here won't do it, but it won't get you anything."

"I'm not Uncle Henry's heir, Mom," Ryan said slowly.

"What? Certainly you are!"

"No, he's not, Vernita," Henry said, a ring of authority in his voice. "Ryan will certainly get something, but he's not my heir. In spite of yourself you raised a good man. Honest. Straight-shooting. We weren't sure you were involved – Ryan didn't think you were – but when we found that Dianne was supposed to have been with her parents that night we decided to tell people I had made him my heir in order to protect her. Dianne will inherit all I have."

"You're lying!" Vernita screamed, the sound bouncing off the concrete walls like flung knives. Clawing her fingers she leapt at Henry, all sanity gone from her face.

Chapter Fourteen

RYAN LOOSED HIS grip on my shoulder and started forward even as Henry put up his fists, but neither of them was needed. Snarling like a wild animal, Vernita fell full length on the floor and lay there twitching as if attached to an electrical current.

Instantly Ryan knelt by his mother, Henry following more slowly and stiffly.

"Mom!" Ryan cried, while Henry held Vernita's head to keep it from banging against the concrete. The froth of white at the corner of her lips turned into a stream and her eyes darted around in their sockets, their expression half fear, half anger – the expression of a trapped and wordless animal. Her left hand flopped around wildly, but aside from an occasional spastic uncontrolled jerk her right one lay motionless. The twitching ended as quickly as it had begun and she relaxed, only her eyes moving. I couldn't tell if she were seeing or not.

"Looks like a stroke," Henry said.

"We've got to get her some help." Ryan gently brushed a stray lock of hair back from her forehead. She might be a murderess, but she was his mother, I kept reminding myself and tried not to think of my own mother's and father's fiery deaths.

"She'll have the best we can get," Henry said, then rose slowly and painfully to his feet. "Sounds like the storm's over. Ryan, take a peek out that trapdoor and see what's going on."

I was afraid that the barn had collapsed on the trap door and we might have to exit through the tunnel Henry said was there – horrible thought! – but when Ryan climbed up and lifted the trap door it opened with only the slightest resistance. A flood of golden light flowed down the steps like water, so bright that Henry blew out the oil lamp.

"It's over," Ryan called, kneeling beside the opening. "Come on up."

Cautiously I poked my head up through the trap

door. Overhead the sky was a brilliant blue vault, barely spotted with strings of thin greyish clouds. Other than a soft zephyr of breeze and the whispering of the pines there was no sound.

The barn had completely vanished save for a carpeting of shredded wood going all the way across the clearing and probably beyond. The pickup lay on its side at the edge of the woods. The car had rolled several times, coming to rest upside down almost at the base of the house steps.

There was no sign of Charley, or of my luggage, or anything else. Except for a smattering of broken wood and debris from the pine trees, the concrete floor of the barn had been swept clean.

Miraculously the house still stood, tall and proud but not undamaged. It seemed as if every window had been broken, for drapes fluttered wanly through the sparkling, teeth-like shards of glass as if waving farewell to the killer winds. Every bit of porch furniture was gone, but one defiant pot of geraniums still hung drunkenly from a tilting pillar. Part of the porch roof was completely gone, while what was left undulated in varying states of support. Two of the posts were broken in half. Heaven only knew what it looked like on the other side.

Ryan bent and took my hands, leading me up from darkness into the watery sunlight, then turned to reach towards Henry. Henry, being Henry, refused the help and climbed out on his own. He smiled when he saw the house.

"Looks like the old place survived. They don't build them like that anymore."

I thought we shouldn't say anything until we saw the interior, until we knew how stable the house was, but kept my mouth closed. Right now we didn't need any negative thoughts.

"That was a stupid thing to do," I said, "making yourself a target like that."

Henry smiled at me with a sweetness that I'd never have imagined. "Better me than you. I knew what was coming."

"You still had all those accidents… She would have killed you, you know."

"She tried."

"And you took that risk just to protect me? You didn't even know me. You didn't even like me!"

"I made a mistake with your mother," he said in slow, painful tones. "I wasn't going to make another mistake with you."

"But to risk your life…"

"Us Wolfes take a lot of killing. We're survivors. And I had Ryan looking out for me." Henry draped a companionable arm around my shoulders. I let it stay there, oddly comforted by his embrace. We simply stood, looking at the old house, and I found myself wishing fervently that it would be all right, that the damage was only cosmetic, that Wolfe House could be brought back to full glory.

Henry was right. We were indeed survivors. So many things full of anger and hatred had happened since I had come to Wolfe House, but I had survived and changed, and was the stronger for it.

"It's a miracle, but my cell works," Ryan said, slipping it back into his pocket. "The twister didn't even get to town and missed the mill entirely. Dave's going to send some people out so we can take Mom to the hospital. I'll bring her up now."

"Are you sure?" Henry asked. "Won't it be safer to have a couple of men help you?"

Ryan shook his head and started down the steps. In a minute or two he was back, struggling up the steps, the limp body of his mother in his arms. Both Henry and I knew better than to offer to help. Some things a son has to do on his own. Gently he laid her on the wind-cleared concrete, standing where he could shade her from the sun.

I would not have recognized her. Vernita's face seemed to be two separate parts clumsily put together. One half was as it had always been, while the other sagged and distorted. A bubbling thread of drool slid from the corner of her mouth.

"I promised her good care," Henry said, removing his arm from my shoulders, then looking Ryan square in the eye, "and she'll get it. She'll never stand trial for what she did."

"I knew she was sick," Ryan said, staring fixedly at the encircling pines. Some were battered and a number lay thrown around like dropped toothpicks, but I would have bet he didn't really see anything. "But I never thought she'd go so far."

He wouldn't look at me, which raised a firestorm of emotion in my heart. Did I want him to look at me? I'd known him only a few days, but was attracted to him as I had never been to anyone, not even my late husband whom I'd known since we were in our teens. His mother had been instrumental in the death of my parents, but should I blame him for that? Could I not?

I looked down at the pathetic husk on the ground. She had my parents killed, had tried to kill my grandfather and had tried to kill me. I could never forgive her. Never. But now she was facing a much higher judgement than either the law or I could ever mete out.

And then there was Ryan.

I looked at Ryan and my entire being twisted. He stood strong and straight, the slight breeze riffling his gingery-brown hair. If it were longer it would probably be very curly. How could I ever have thought him unhandsome? He was the best looking man I had ever seen.

As if aware of my gaze he looked back at me and the world seemed to shift on its axis. It took every ounce of will I had to keep from running into his arms.

"Henry… Grandfather..." I said slowly, "I want to go back to California."

Epilogue

THE PLANE CIRCLED lazily over the seemingly unending sea of pine trees, then the forest below turned into urban sprawl and we finally touched down at the Longview airport. It had been six months – six of the longest months of my life – since I had flown away from that same airport with nothing but the wallet that had luckily been in my pocket and a heavy heart.

Decisions are never easy, especially when they are life changing. But – sometimes what we fear must be faced up to with courage, even when we know that our lives will never be the same again.

The plane dropped lower, and my heart began to pound.

Since leaving the wounded Wolfe House I had talked to Henry almost every day, ostensibly about whether or not we would continue to do the biography, though we both knew it was only an excuse. That book was, at least for the foreseeable future, dead in the water.

After the first week or so I had also talked to Ryan, when more often than not Henry would hand me off to him. Henry was determined that I should inherit, and equally as determined that I should know something of the business and that Ryan, who was pretty much running the place, should teach me. A sensible idea, but more than a little harrowing.

At first Ryan's and my conversations had been stilted things, focused only on business, but with an amazing rapidity they had softened into a kind of friendship and mutual respect.

We did not talk of his mother, or her actions. Henry told me what happened. He had been right – no charges would ever be filed against Vernita. She was in a good nursing home and would never leave it. Her body lived in a state of near total paralysis; her mind – well, no one knew what she was aware of, if anything, or if she were even in there at all.

Which, if you think about it, could be the cruelest punishment of all.

Wolfe House had survived the storm well. The porch roof had been easily rebuilt and new furniture bought. There had been some slight damage inside due to the broken windows, but that too had been easy to fix. Enough shingles had been ripped away to dictate a new roof, but miracle of miracles, the stained glass roof over the stairwell had not been broken.

Amazingly, neither had the windows in my mother's room. It was the only room in the house that had survived completely intact.

The real surprise was in Vernita's room. No one had been allowed in there while she was in residence, and both Henry and Ryan were amazed at what they found. This was not the room of a housekeeper, nor even a shirttail relative; Vernita's room was suitable for an anointed queen. Luxurious fabrics, glorious antique furniture, expensive accessories... a setting fit for the queen of Wolfe House.

They also found my mother's jewelry – her pearls, the diamond earrings, the pieces she treasured she had told me about – and the red spinel ring. It was as incredible as Mother had described it. Henry had all her pieces and the portrait sent to me by special courier. I loved them, cried over them, but even after I had them something was lacking, and I was afraid to admit even to myself what it was.

It took several months before I could accept that I had to return to Wolfe House... and why. The ostensible reason was that as future owner of the mill – and Henry's other companies – there were things I had to learn, papers I had to sign in person. The other reason... Was it too late? Or totally irrelevant? I didn't know, and the only way I could find out was to go.

Finally we landed. In my hyper-tense state getting off the plane, reclaiming my bag and getting out of the security area seemed to take longer than the flight. Towing my overloaded suitcase behind me, I walked out into the main hall.

Ryan was there, as I had known he would be. He

was impeccably dressed, as always, looking as if he had escaped from the pages of GQ. His hair was slightly rumpled, and he wore no sunglasses, so I could see all of his face and most especially his eyes. They were warm and welcoming, but guarded. I suppose mine were, too.

For one long moment we simply stared at each other as the bustle of the airport swirled around us like a tide.

Then he held out his arms and, dropping my suitcase, I ran into them, truly, finally, home at last.

About the Author

Janis Susan May is a seventh-generation Texan and a third-generation wordsmith who writes mysteries as Janis Patterson, romances and other things as Janis Susan May, children's books as Janis Susan Patterson and scholarly works as J.S.M. Patterson.

Formerly an actress and singer, a talent agent and Supervisor of Accessioning for a bio-genetic DNA testing lab, Janis has also been editor-in-chief of two multi-magazine publishing groups. She founded and was the original editor of The Newsletter of the North Texas Chapter of the American Research Center in Egypt, which for the nine years of her reign was the international organization's only monthly publication. Long interested in Egyptology, she was one of the founders of the North Texas chapter and was the closing speaker for the ARCE International Conference in Boston in 2005.

Janis married for the first time when most of her contemporaries were becoming grandmothers. Her husband, a handsome Navy Captain several years younger than she, even proposed in a moonlit garden in Egypt. Janis and her husband live in Texas with an assortment of rescued furbabies.

www.JanisSusanMay.com

Devil's Promenade
A World of Gothic: United States
by Alicia Dean

Chapter One

I PEERED THROUGH THE snow-dusted windshield at the large house looming in the evening dusk, and an unwarranted shiver of foreboding washed over my flesh.

From behind the wheel, my driver, Rita, made a sound that was somewhere between a squeak of trepidation and a sigh of admiration. "It's huge. And gorgeous, but kind of creepy, don't you think?" Her eyes were big and round behind the lenses of her black cat-eye frames.

"It is indeed." The sprawling structure was a combination of Southern plantation and Greek revival architecture; painted white and trimmed in a darker colored molding—perhaps forest green. The exact color was difficult to make out in the descending dusk. Narrow, darkened floor-to-ceiling windows peeked from between a portico of six Doric columns. Hanging by chains above the porch, a wooden board flapped in the icy wind. *Spook Light Bed and Breakfast.* The sign should have been welcoming, yet apprehension clawed at my heart.

Might as well get over that silliness. This would be my home for the next two weeks while I learned all I could about the Hornet Spook Light. The phenomenon, also known as the Tri-State Spook Light, Joplin Spook Light, Devil's Jack-O-Lantern, and a few other nicknames, had supposedly been spotted multiple times over the last few centuries in this area, at the border of Oklahoma, Missouri, and Kansas. I was here to do research for my book—*The Myth of Otherworldly Occurrences.* I chuckled and rolled my eyes. The only thing *otherworldly* about this place was its location thousands of miles from my warm, sunny home in Florida.

I glanced at Rita. Frizzy hair surrounded an oval face that seemed to have paled further since we arrived at the mansion. "Thank you for the ride. It was nice getting to know you." My publisher had sent Rita to pick me up at the airport in Joplin and drive me to my destination in Quapaw, Oklahoma. She was friendly and chatty, and the forty-five minute trip had flown by quickly. I looked back out the window at the imposing structure. Maybe it had flown by a little too quickly.

I reached for the door handle, but hesitated, filled by an odd reluctance. I wanted to stay within the warm confines of the SUV, say to heck with the book, return the advance I'd received, and forget I'd ever been to the area known as Devil's Promenade.

But, writing paid the bills. I needed to suck it up and get on with it. Besides, the last place I wanted to be right now was home, at least until Valentine's Day—and the wedding—were over.

Rita squeezed my arm through my thick coat, bringing my attention back to her. "I enjoyed getting to know you too, Cami." She popped the back lift gate with the inside lever, letting in a blast of icy air. "I'll help with your luggage."

"No, I've got it. No sense in both of us freezing to death." I handed her a tip, slipped on my gloves, and then, bracing myself, opened the door. Cold wind buffeted me. I had to struggle to climb out of the car. Boots crunching over the snow, I hurried to the back and grabbed my rolling suitcase and overnight bag. I'd packed light. The website said laundry facilities were available, so I saw no point in lugging an entire two-week wardrobe.

Head down, I tromped through the snow, shivering even in my warm coat as I tugged my case along the path. Other than the dim light glowing from the porch and the three-quarter moon drifting in the inky sky, the evening throbbed with a blackness deeper than any I'd ever experienced. Murky silence pressed around me. I'd never heard such an absence of sound, never seen—no, *felt*—such darkness.

I was a few feet from the steps when the sound of a throaty bark, followed by a high-pitched keening broke the stillness. Before the noise abated, another identical howl rose.

My footsteps halted, my knees weakening. What was that? Dogs? Coyotes? A shudder raced over my spine. At home in Miami, I didn't encounter wild animals, other than the occasional feral cat. The thought of being in close proximity with dangerous wildlife was completely unexpected—and alarming. I glanced around at the nearby woods.

How close were the creatures? Close enough to

lunge, knock me to the ground, sink their sharp teeth into my throat, gouge my flesh until blood spurted in a red torrent, draining my life as I screamed in agonized terror...?

I vigorously shook my head. *Stop it, Cami.* Geez. Where had that thought come from? For such a pragmatic person, I was certainly entertaining fanciful notions.

Shifting the strap of my purse and carryall higher on my shoulder, I ascended the stairs to the porch. I reached out a gloved hand for the brass knocker, but before I touched it, the door swung open.

An attractive middle-aged woman, blonde hair piled atop her head in a messy, yet somehow sophisticated bun, smiled warmly from inside the doorway. Behind her, dim lighting glowed in a foyer elegantly appointed in gold and ivory.

"You must be Camille Burditt. I'm Loretta Delgado, welcome to Spook Light Bed and Breakfast." She stepped back and extended a welcoming arm. "Please, come in, I'm sure you're frozen solid."

"Yes, thank you," I managed through chattering teeth.

I started to step forward and something cold—colder than the frigid February air—brushed along my nape beneath my snow-dampened hair. I gasped and whirled, looking back out into the night. A brief glow penetrated the snowy dusk, then was gone.

"Are you okay, dear?"

It took a moment to respond, but I nodded, attempting to make sense of what had just happened. Tremors vibrated through my stomach, and I swallowed a knot of fear. Was that the spook light? No, of course it wasn't. The house sat several yards back from the road where the light had been seen—well, where people *claimed* they'd seen it. Those alleged sightings had been between the hours of ten p.m. and sunrise. This was much too early. So, what had I seen? Not a ghost. Specters didn't exist, except in the imaginings of weak-minded people who needed something to believe in.

Nothing, that's what I'd seen. I was just exhausted and freaked out by the remote wildness of my surroundings. But I could have sworn…

Nothing, it was nothing.

I hurried across the threshold, breathing a sigh of relief when the heavy oak door shut out the blackness, the eerie sounds, and the spot where I'd witnessed the inexplicable glow that was positively, definitely and for certain, *not* a ghost.

Coming September 8, 2016:

Raven of Blackthorn Manor

A World of Gothic: Ireland

by Gemma Juliana

Chapter One

I'LL NEVER FORGET my first glimpse of Raventhorn Manor. It stood bold and gaunt amidst the early winter landscape, its presence as bleakly intimidating as that of any person I've ever feared.

I suspected it was taking stock of me, too, and somehow it managed to make me aware that, as surely as it embedded itself in the very essence of my being, my life would change forever as a result of our encounter.

A chill wind permeated the air and found its way into the car as the light was sucked from the day. I reached for the knob that regulated heat and turned it to full blast, then snuggled deeper into my black leather jacket.

As I reached for my water bottle, the blood-red fiery stone in my ring caught my attention. It was a large round finely-faceted spinel set in gold. I wore it on my middle finger, and thought of it as a good luck talisman.

Perhaps it wanted to remind me to expect good luck and not to become too morbid.

"You've been very quiet since we left Kilkenny," Rick Riordan observed, casting a quick glance sideways at me from the driver's seat. "Not your usual chatty self. What gives?"

"I'm hardly chatty at the best of times," I retorted, wishing my moods weren't so easily read by others. He was right, of course. Terrifying nightmares for three nights straight had left my nerves raw and edgy. The only common threads were isolation, a menacing presence I couldn't identify, and the knowledge I was in danger. As we drew closer to Blackthorn Manor my pulse quickened. "Darkness will be upon us soon."

"You don't sound particularly thrilled." He pulled the car over into the muddy entrance of a farmer's gateway, and the great manor on the hill mocked me. "This is huge, Morgana. The biggest gig you've ever scored. I thought you'd be elated."

"I've had a headache all afternoon, as if something oppressive is pounding on my head."

"Try again," he smirked, reaching for a bottle of soda and taking a good long drink. "You'll have to do better than that."

I sighed, then pulled the hairclip out of my thick black hair. Swirling it all into a top knot, I stabbed the clip back into it and crossed my arms over my chest. I didn't dare meet his eyes. He knew me too well.

"I wish you could stay at the manor, too," I finally admitted, feeling foolish. "I've had some unsettling nightmares for the last few days."

"The letter was adamant that you must go alone." Rick resumed driving and took an unexpected curve a little too fast. As we rounded the bend, fog started forming in the road, and a flock of ghostly white sheep trotted along in front of us. "Bloody hell, what next!"

"Look at all the gnarled and twisted trees. Ireland must have the market cornered on haunting trees. I've never seen so many."

"They're hardly as dangerous as these twisting hairpin roads. They hardly qualify to be called roads. Some are little more than paths." Rick inched along on the isolated stretch and continued heading south. "I've never prayed so hard that we don't run into oncoming traffic."

"I recognize some yews and hemlock trees, but what

are those stunted ones that aren't more than about twelve feet tall? They're particularly warped looking."

"Blackthorns." He waited for it to sink in. "Very powerful magic. It's the tree of the Morrighan, goddess of war and bloodshed."

"Lovely." I squeezed my weary eyes shut. *What have I gotten myself into?* "I suppose there'll be plenty of them where I'm going."

"No doubt." We drove through the ground fog in silence as darkness descended. Silver lined the edges of a black cloud looming before us as it cloaked the moon.

"Feels like we're at the ends of the earth," I whispered.

"Look, you'll be fine," Rick tried to assure me. "I'll be with the rest of the film crew on the haunted beach about two hours away. If you can't stand it, call and I'll come for you early. Otherwise, I'll be back for you in a week."

He may as well have said he'd be back next year. The prospect of spending a week at the most haunted property in Ireland without my team, or even a friend, was rattling my cage.

"Why do you think Sir Blackthorn wouldn't let

anyone else come?"

"It's odd, but what's the worst that can happen? The property has a horrible history, but nothing evil has actually happened to anyone lately, right?" Rick didn't sound as sure of himself as he'd have me think.

"Who knows?" Edginess laced my words. "According to my research, there have been plenty of deaths on that land over the years. And worse, several people have vanished into thin air."

"Your ability to see and communicate with ghosts will keep you safe," Rick announced. "You're the perfect person to receive this invitation. Maybe you can pave the way for us to film a documentary before we fly home."

"Don't count on it," I retorted, knowing that would not be an option.

Suddenly the moon cleared the black cloud that had repressed its light and cast a silver sheen over the land. It was eerie and magnificent all at once. Signs announced that a small town was just ahead.

"That must be the town we go through." I pointed. "Then take the beach road. The estate is on the west side of the peninsula just a little way down. I saw the manor house looming over that way a few miles back."

Within minutes, we'd crossed through the heart of the village and came out the other end. The beach road was well sign-posted.

Isolated was an understatement.

The very air grew oppressive as a sense of impending doom descended over me. My heart pounded and fear churned in my gut. At the same time there was a realization that my time at Blackthorn Manor was inevitable.

A gate bell allowed Rick to communicate with someone somewhere on the other side of the tall iron gates. In moments, they swung open on squeaky hinges. We entered and drove up the curved drive. Silhouettes of twisted trees thrust their boughs at wild angles like old hags dancing in the dark of the moon. Blackthorns, no doubt.

Glittering light in what seemed like a hundred lead pane windows greeted us farther up. The house was immense, Gothic spires and arches dominating the landscape. Welcoming it was not. I shuddered.

Rick pulled the car to a stop at the front steps. "I'll go ring the bell, then get your bag."

I watched his long-legged familiar figure take the

steps two at a time. Moments after he rang the bell, one of the doors cracked open, and golden light poured out onto the steps. He spoke briefly with someone, then came back to the car and fetched my roll-wheel bag.

Taking my arm, he led me up to the door.

"Weird housekeeper," he whispered in my ear, then all but thrust me into the foyer. "Have fun," and he was bolting down the steps to the car, which took off amidst a burst of flying gravel.

I stared at the gargoyle-like features of the stout older woman whose eyes were fixed on me.

"And you're…?" Her voice was inhospitable and her eyes distrusting.

"Morgana Pierce." I stammered. "I'm here for a week at the invitation of Sir Blackthorn."

"He's turned in for the night and said nothing about a guest." She fixed her blank stare on me again. "Nothing."

I reached into my handbag and withdrew the letter I'd received out of the blue three days earlier. It was typed on the letterhead of this fine manor house and signed by him. I held it out for her to inspect.

She looked it over carefully. "Hmmm." She was none too pleased at having to make a decision like this on her own. "It's not like the master to leave me in the dark… this is very disturbing. Follow me, Ms. Pierce. I'll show you to a guest room for the night. Sir Blackthorn must determine what to do about you in the morning."

As I followed the woman across the large elegant entrance hall and up the marble staircase, I stopped dead while rounding the corner to a long hallway.

A large portrait of a regal woman mocked me. She could be my identical twin.

Made in the USA
Monee, IL
18 January 2023